A BUZZ BOOK

ST. MARTIN'S PRESS ≈ NEW YORK

nixoncarver

mark maxwell

Portions of this work were previously published in *Passages North*.

nixoncarver. Copyright © 1998 by Mark Maxwell. All rights reserved. Printed in the United States of America. No part of this book may be used or reproduced in any manner whatsoever without written permission except in the case of brief quotations embodied in critical articles or reviews. For information, address A Buzz Book for St. Martin's Press, 175 Fifth Avenue, New York, N.Y. 10010.

design by maureen troy

Library of Congress Cataloging-in-Publication Data

Maxwell, Mark,
    nixoncarver / Mark Maxwell. — 1st ed.
        p.   cm. — (Buzz books)
    ISBN 0-312-18146-9
    1. Carver, Raymond—Fiction.   2. Nixon, Richard M. (Richard Milhous), 1913–1994 —Fiction. I. Title. II. Series : Buzz books (Series)
PS3563.A922N58   1998
813'.54—dc21   97-40068
                                              CIP

Web site http://www.buzzmag.com

First Buzz Books Edition: February 1998

10 9 8 7 6 5 4 3 2 1

For Elizabeth, who saved my life

contents

author's note

nixoncarver is a work of fiction. While it shares certain facts with the lives of Richard Nixon and Raymond Carver, the work is in no way an attempt to capture the factual truth about them, their friends, families or colleagues. I have significantly altered the facts to suit my purpose, which was to simultaneously perpetuate and alter the common myths about Nixon and Carver. In writing *nixoncarver* I created composite characters and completely invented situations which never occurred in real life and people who never existed. Even though certain public figures have been identified, their characterizations and the events depicted concerning them are entirely fictional. Nothing in this book, therefore, should be read as factual.

The loose framework for *nixoncarver*'s events was derived from a variety of sources including biographies, oral histories, essays, poems, letters, and memos. Wherever possible I have relied on Richard Nixon's public papers and his autobiography. Nixon's "memos" included in the work are either entirely fictional or fictional composites of actual public records. Some scenes were inspired by events depicted in Raymond Carver's poetry. I have tried to make direct references to these poems by title in the context of the scenes which were inspired by them, but it wasn't always possible. Therefore, I would like to acknowledge "The Ashtray," "A Haircut," "The Autopsy Room," "My

Dad's Wallet," "Drinking While Driving," "The Kitchen," "Photograph of My Father in His Twenty-Second Year," and the essay "Fires."

special thanks

Scott Anderson
Carol Anshaw
Bill Artz
Phyllis Barber
Jim Fitzgerald
Douglas Glover
Elizabeth Kruse
Michael Kruse
Richard Lanis

Stephen Manella
Maria Mondragon
Moonshine
Anthony Oakson
Laurie Rossi
Sharon Sheehe Stark
Dale Worsley
Elizabeth Ziemska

nixoncarver

Greetings

As I watch the rising tide from my rocky perch, I'm thinking of greeting cards. The kind with an image of the setting sun and a silhouette of two lovers walking hand in hand. Above the lovers' heads, in the distance, a lone seagull soars. Inside, the card says something in fancy script lettering about how the tide can erase the barriers between our worlds.

If I don't get off this rock, I know the tidewater will reach me, wrap itself around me, and eventually pass me by. Up the beach a swarm of gulls ambushes a decaying carcass of some sort. The scavengers peck at their prey and caw and slap at each other with their wings. One of them sits proud atop a hunk of rotting flesh, surveying his competition. He sighs at the lack of challenge before him, then looks in my direction as if to tempt me. Go ahead, I dare you, his sneer says.

Down the coast, south of here, at San Clemente, Richard Nixon's ocean view is much like the one I'm looking at. A large picture window in his office faces the roaring seascape, but Nixon's leather reading chair is turned with its back to the window. He doesn't want his thoughts interrupted by the crash of a wave or the call of a seagull. Scowling in his chair, he scribbles on a yellow legal pad and then mutters something to himself, something like: "I don't even deserve my clothes."

And somewhere up the coast to the north in Port Angeles, Washington, Ray Carver, the legendary American poet, sits in his straight-backed typing chair with a pillow under his ass to ease his swelling hemorrhoids. There are cancer cells multiplying in his lungs as he pecks away at his Smith Corona, writing his poems. Every day the poems come. Little gems he didn't know he had in him. Gifts from someplace. His desk, unlike Nixon's, faces the window, which faces the sea. Now and then he pauses and stares out blankly, wondering who sent him these gifts, waiting for the chair to be yanked out from under him one final time. Then back to the typewriter he goes, writing and then writing some more.

Nixon has just resigned his position as leader of the free world, and Carver has just found out he needs his left lung removed. When the ex-president tires of waging lawsuits and the writer runs out of malignant metaphors, they find themselves out walking the Pacific coastline they share, contemplating the cards they've been dealt in these lives they've led.

Nixon heads north from San Clemente with no particular destination. He wanders up the beach into a mist, his own foggy past fading behind him as he walks on, hunched, but still proud somehow. Carver heads south from Port Angeles, searching for a hyperbolic image in the grains of sand at his feet as the cancer cells multiply in his chest.

They've been walking for days, these two men—this poet and this politician. One foot in front of the other—lifting, moving, placing—step after step. I am between them on my rock, watching and waiting. I am between them. Me and what's left of the shoreline they've traveled—only a few footsteps of the America they once owned.

When I see them emerge out of the lifting fog like ghosts, I know I have been waiting here my whole life for these two men, waiting for their paths to cross and hoping that something might bring them to greet each other here on this rocky coast.

One hand reaches across the sand for the other. The mist seems to hang perfectly still between them. The fog stops swirling up the shore. The crest of every wave is frozen. Their hands hover, about to clasp, about to join their two worlds.

When their hands finally meet, there's something soft in their grip. Something dry and soft. It's not the firm, sticky handshake of two men searching each other's palms for weapons. It's a greeting of condolences, a greeting that erases the space between them.

Ray Carver points into the thick air and says, "Fine day, isn't it?"

Nixon nods. He wants to say, I was president once, and now everyone hates me. But he sees immediately that this is irrelevant. "My name's Dick," is all he says, as if he thinks Ray may not recognize him.

Ray says, "Nice to meet you, Dick." They're two old friends just playing at meeting each other for the first time.

They stand in silence in the sand—Ray occasionally splashing in the water, Dick a few safe footsteps from the rising tide.

Ray bends to pick up a stone and skips it into an oncoming wave. "How's the wife?" Ray asks.

"Still in the hospital," Dick tells him. "She can't even talk out of the left side of her mouth anymore. Slurs all of her damn words like an old drunk."

"I'm still dying," Ray says with an odd Buddha smirk on his lips.

"I thought so," says Dick. "You've got that look about you."

"You would know."

"You better believe it." Dick spots a good flat skipping stone. He bends, picks it up, and hands it to Ray. "The other day after I visited Pat in the hospital, I went home, took everything out of her closet, and then curled up in a ball in the corner and screamed into a pillow for hours. I screamed until I went hoarse," Dick says. "Then my daughter came over and fixed me dinner. But I couldn't eat a thing."

"I've been there," says Ray.

"And then even a few days later," Dick says, "I still didn't feel any better. Pat's still limp and lifeless in her hospital bed, but instead of going back into the closet, I found myself putting on a pair of shoes and going for a stroll. I must have walked a couple hundred miles before you showed up."

"It's the same way with me," says Ray. "Same damn thing."

They turn and look inland, away from the foggy coast, to places where there are no fault lines threatening to separate them from the mainland and send them adrift.

Finally, they head north toward Ray's place. For a minute, I look away and let them walk on without me. But I can't stand it. Quietly, I turn back and see them up the beach. They're leaning up against a couple of big rocks, and they're waiting. They're waiting for me this time.

From somewhere up in the gray air, a seagull calls.

They wave me toward them and smile at each other. They're being smug, like they've taught me a lesson or something, but I don't mind. Let them think what they want. Just so I can tag along for a while and see what becomes of them.

Nine Lives

When Dick was too small to understand what dreams meant, he used to let himself dream of bluebirds fluttering out of his mother's asshole. The clean, winking red eye between his mother's soft, fleshy cheeks would open and close under the pressure of her fingertips. And the baby bluebirds would poke their wet little heads out, beak first, eyes shut. They'd be squawking up a storm as their crusty eyes blinked opened. Then they'd wiggle their little bird shoulders through and finally their wings, which they'd flap anxiously until they were airborne. Then the next one would pop out. And so on.

Little Dickie would awake, sweating. Always sweating. And his parents would come to him. Mother first, followed by the kalumphing footsteps of Pa.

"He's had another nightmare," Mother would say.

"Were you dreaming of Satan's fires again, son?" Pa would ask. "Well, don't worry, boy. There ain't a good Quaker alive that's gotta worry about old Satan coming to visit."

"He's just a child," Mother would say. "You'll give him more nightmares, Frank."

"Don't you worry, boy. Go back to sleep. It's late."

Then Mother would tuck the blankets in around Dick's lumpy little frame, and Father would muss Dick's sweat-slicked hair.

As they left his bedside and walked toward his doorway, he

wanted to call out to them, ask them not to leave him, ask them to pray with him. And most of all he wanted to apologize for the dream he'd had and the other dreams he would let himself have as soon as he fell back to sleep. But he didn't call after them. He couldn't. He was on his own now—a big boy, out of the womb, ready for the world.

He just pulled the sheets up to his chin and watched as they retreated down the narrow hall, the light fading as they went.

At breakfast they ate oatmeal. Every day.

Dick, now old enough to be out of his sissy high chair, is learning the hows and whys of spoon-feeding himself. He struggles the slop into his awaiting mouth, a gaping hole in the middle of his large, curly-haired head. A crusty layer of snot runs down the back of his throat. A bad-breathed little tyke, but it's nothing a good bowl of gluey oatmeal can't fix.

Elbows not yet high enough to reach the tabletop, young Richard peeks over the horizon of his steaming bowl, reaches a stubby fistful of spoon up over the edge, submerges the shining instrument into the gray gruel, and scoops a hearty mouthful. A teetering wobble of drippy sludge makes its way to the middle of his face. Tentatively, he blows, ever so gentle. Richard plunges the spoon into that hole, tongue and mouth-roof trapping the spoon and then releasing the pressure just enough to allow for a snug withdrawal—a momentary shiver of heat-pain and sweet delight.

The boy swallows. Acids and biles churn and begin to transform God's golden grain into a lumpy brown mess, which by tomorrow morning, alone in the outhouse, Richard will try to wipe clean from his tiny little ass—a place too dirty for bluebirds.

As the first spoonful of oatmeal begins its long journey, Richard, little more than a puke-faced twerp, wipes the spoon across his lips, making sure to scrape away every trace of food from the corners and crevices—a trick his mother taught him when he was still in his high chair. Spoon, swallow, swipe.

"Look, Mom. Look! He's doing it again. Richard's doing that thing with his spoon, Mom! You want I should spank him for you?" says Richard's older brother Harold.

"Harold, he's just a child. Leave him alone. Richard dear, if you want to wipe the spoon across your lips, it's okay. You pay no attention to your brother. And Harold, he's just learning how. He likes the way it feels to be clean. Is that so terrible?"

Clean. That's the way Richard liked it, all right. Squeaky clean. Get rid of my smelly breath. Get rid of this crud in my butthole. Make me human, Momma. Straighten my hair. Plug up my sweat glands. Shrink my big dumb forehead. I'm an ape, Momma. How can anyone love an ape?

Once a week, Hannah gives the child a warm bath. She heats water in a kettle over the fire in the kitchen. She fills his little tub, strands of dark hair falling out of her bun. It's Richard's fault her hair is a mess, Richard's fault she's up to her elbows in his grime.

Hannah lifts her son into his little tub, gently testing the water temperature with his bare bottom. He never complains. He likes it hot. The hotter the better. The steam rises around him. He wants to splash like any other little boy—big wavy splashes, bigger than any Harold could make. Harold, that piss-faced brother of his. But Richard resists the urge to navigate tidal waves. He sits still and gazes into the steam as his mother soaks a dish towel and drags it across his slippery little back.

One day, Richard will be expected to bathe himself, no doubt. Harold takes his bath alone—cold baths in the same big tub Father uses, with the door closed. Richard wonders if his mother ever bathed Harold. Or had Harold been born knowing how to clean himself? He wonders too if she ever hummed in Harold's ear. The lilting caress of her rhythms dances its way through the hot misty cloud and washes over Richard as Hannah reaches underneath him. A week's worth of crud down there. She wipes him with the dish towel.

. . .

On Sundays after church, Frank Nixon always smoked a cigar. In his rocker in the corner, he rolled the cigar between thumb and forefinger, licking its tip. He looked to Richard like he was daring someone to challenge him. He looked like a big man, a father in his favorite chair, on a Sunday, not to be disturbed. A successful man.

But outside in the fields, Frank Nixon's pathetic little crops strangled one another, withered, and collapsed. Dusty Yorba Linda earth laughed at the fool and his cigar and his smelly-assed little son.

"Beware the future, my boy," Frank says to Harold, chewing on the smoldering brown stub in the corner of his mouth. "I once saw a man kill a chicken in cold blood. It weren't even an eatin' chicken. Just some stray, scraggly little bastard that crossed the wrong path." Pa pauses for emphasis, eyes Harold through the smoke. Richard listens from a distant corner.

"You know why that son of a bitch killed that chicken? I'll tell you why. 'Cause he didn't know how to count, that's why. You see what I'm saying, boy? The future never arrives." He pauses again. "And only a cat has nine lives."

Harold nods and Richard wonders how long it will be before his father will include him in this conspiracy. Or maybe it isn't a conspiracy at all. Maybe dumb-as-shit Harold didn't know what the hell Father was talking about either. Maybe Richard is the only one on planet earth who will see through Frank Nixon's cigar-smoke philosophies. Maybe someday Harold will still be nodding, pretending to get it, but only Richard would see that counting has nothing whatsoever to do with killing a chicken. But if there was something to it, and Harold did understand it, why was Richard so dense? When would he be old enough to get it? When would he be old enough to wish he had nine lives?

Forty Stitches

The sky was clear, the sun warm. But there was something gray hovering over the afternoon. A bass cut the surface of the water, mocking Ray Carver and his old man on their raft with their fishing poles in hand. Bullfrogs croaked a song on nearby lily pads, and somewhere out of sight, a turtle retreated into itself.

Ray's father hawked up a loogie and sent it sailing in a masterful arc through the still spring air. Two ducks scurried toward the wad of phlegm, thinking it might be something edible. One nibbled at it and then thought better of it. Ray's father took a swig of the hair of the dog. Ray stared out at the water, waiting for a bite on his line. Beside him, his father cursed their lousy luck and changed bait.

Ray Senior fumbled with the hook, his eyes intent. The old man's wide thumbs trembled as he crammed the hook with worms. It didn't take much for the hook to find its way into Ray Senior's fleshy thumb—a slight slip, a momentary distraction, the breeze kicking the smells of last night's binge back up into his face. The thumb bled plenty, as always. Ray's dad shook the hand out, swore, and sucked his own blood.

"I suppose you think this is funny," Ray's dad said, holding up the thumb. "I suppose you think I deserve this."

· · ·

The night before Ray had found his father in the kitchen with a strange toothless woman on his lap. Actually she wasn't completely toothless, but she wasn't completely toothed either. She was sitting on Ray's father's lap, smoking a cigarette and blowing smoke into Ray's father's mouth. They were kissing, his father and this toothless woman. She'd take a drag off her cigarette, kiss Ray's father, and blow the smoke into Ray's father's mouth while they kissed. When she was out of smoke, she'd pull away, and Ray's father would blow the smoke out through his nose. The toothless woman giggled and kissed Ray's father some more.

Ray had watched them from the kitchen window for a while. They were drinking whiskey out of coffee mugs and playing this game with the cigarette smoke. And once in a while, Ray's father would squeeze the woman's breast and lick the nipple area right through her shirt. Ray couldn't tell from the window if the woman was wearing a bra or not. His mother was in the bedroom, no doubt, while this was going on in her kitchen. She'd be crying, but by the next day, she'd be burning eggs and flapjacks on the stove again.

The fish weren't biting, so Ray reeled his line in, took off his shirt, and made ready to jump off the pier for a swim. His father said, "Where the hell do you think you're going?"

"I'm hot," Ray said. "I thought I'd swim some."

His father grumbled but said nothing, and as Ray stepped to the edge of the pier, he slipped. The pain was delayed, but even before it struck, Ray was aware of something sharp entering his skin. A jagged piece of wood, a rusty nail, something. Whatever it was, it dug in and held on, and as Ray's momentum carried him forward into the water, he felt his flesh rip. He sank to the mucky bottom of the lake, flailing as the pain announced itself. In his panic, Ray seemed to have forgotten how to swim. He was screaming under the water, but there was no sound. Nothing came out of him but bubbles. Bubbles and blood. When Ray finally bobbed to the surface, he splashed frantically in three directions at once and started hollering for his father who was most certainly sucking the last few drops out of another bottle of Rhinelander.

Ray Senior. turned to his son then and said, "What the hell is your problem now?"

Somehow the voice put him at ease and he stopped flailing. But when Ray looked down in the direction of the pain, he could see the water turning darker around him in patchy swirls. "My leg," he shouted. "I think I cut my leg."

Ray's dad shook his head, turned his lips into an upside-down smirk of disgust, and said in his hangover voice, "Swim your ass over here and I'll take a look."

Ray managed to splash his way back up onto the pier and when he saw the damage he'd done to his leg, the horizon turned over a couple of times on him. The leg looked like someone had taken a meat hook to it. His father poked around into the cut.

"My oh my," his father said with a whistle. "That's a beauty. You really did it this time, boy. We're going to have to get you to the hospital and see if they can sew you back together."

The world rocked back into place and left Ray feeling like he'd just gotten off a ride at the fairgrounds. He wanted to vomit, but he swallowed hard instead. "How we gonna get to the hospital from here?" he managed.

His dad said, "Well, boy, you're going to have to pretend you're a man for once. We'll get you back to the shoreline. Then you'll hoist your bloody little self up and we'll walk to the road. If we can flag down a car, that means God loves you, boy. But I wouldn't count on it, cause if God really loved you, we'd have a car of our own, wouldn't we? If we don't see no car on the road, I guess that means we're walking."

"But, Dad, it's eight or nine miles to the hospital."

"Well, if worse comes to worse, I leave you a few of my beers and you can sit on the roadside and tie on your first drunk while I go get help. But you ain't gonna bleed to death, so don't be such a woman about it."

By now the pain was already unbearable. It was worse when Ray looked at the cut, of course, but he couldn't help himself. As disgusting as it was, there was something incredible about being able to see inside your own body like that. To see the way things worked in there, one part dependent on the others. His father took off his T-shirt and wrapped it around Ray's wound. It was a bloody mess of muscle and tendon and gashed flesh. The blood just kept coming. There was no stopping it.

"C'mon, Junior," Ray's father said, offering an arm to lean on.

"It hurts, Dad."

"I'm sure it does from the looks of it. But it ain't gonna stop hurting till we get you to the hospital, so just focus on that for right now."

Ray hopped alongside his father, wincing and making a snake sound every time he accidentally put pressure on the leg. His father was holding him tight and looking pretty sober, considering. They made their way to the road through a rocky path that led up a slight hill through the trees. It was the shortest route but it was a bit overgrown with bramble and such. Ray's father held the branches back out of Ray's way as they navigated.

At one point, near the top, Ray Senior stopped to check his son's leg. He pulled back the soaked T-shirt and took a close look. He rubbed his chin. Ray was trying to see too, but his father said, "Turn your head, boy. Your face is in my light. I can't see a damn thing with that big noggin of yours blocking out the sun. It's like a damn eclipse down here."

Ray was young, probably only ten or eleven at the time. But Ray knew his father better than he knew himself, and there was something in the old man's voice that sounded like nothing Ray had ever heard before. The words were his father's words all right, but there was something in them Ray didn't recognize. It wasn't panic or fear exactly. But something like that. His father looked up at him. "What are you looking at, Junior? I thought I told you to turn that big head of yours."

That's when Ray Senior picked his son up off the ground like a rag doll—swooped him up in one quick motion before Ray could even protest. There in his father's arms for the first time in who knows how long, Ray said, "What are you doing, Dad?"

"I'm going to have to carry you over the top of the ridge, Son. Be still now. We're almost there."

The old man's face was drained. White as a ghost, as they say. He huffed up the ridge. Ray wrapped his arms around his father's neck. The leg was bad. There was no doubt about it. It was written all over his father's face. It was written in the scrunched lines on his forehead and the sparse stubble on his chin. And it was written in his mouth. Instead of his usual tight-lipped frown, the old man's mouth hung open as he panted up the hill, squeezing his son tight against him.

Young Junior saw his father's fear, but for some reason, he himself wasn't afraid anymore at all. In fact, now that he knew just how bad the leg was, a weight seemed to have been lifted off him. There was nothing he could do about it. It was bad, and that was that. Even the pain seemed to be subsiding, giving itself over to a kind of relaxed numbness.

At the top of the hill, Ray's dad gently set his son down on a flat roadside boulder. "Sit still," he said. "And don't mess with that rag. I got it tied good and tight and I don't want you to loosen it up, you hear?"

Ray nodded. But he was fading now. He slumped against a tree. His father was walking up the road a bit. He would flag down a car. There would be a car. And he would flag it down. Then they'd go to the hospital. Maybe everything would be okay. The doctors would fix Ray's leg. And afterwards, Ray would get to stay home from school for a few days and maybe his father would sit by the side of his bed and do magic tricks for him. He'd pull a nickel out of Ray's ear, make a penny disappear into thin air. He'd make magic with both of them—the penny and the nickel. And for a few days everything would be all right. It would be worth thirty or forty stitches. It would be worth it.

Kiss

There were times when Dick didn't know what to say. It was rare, but when it happened, he was paralyzed by his own silence. Like the time when Arthur kissed him. Arthur was only four years old at the time. Dick was eight. It was when Arthur had first taken ill and Dick and Harold were being sent off to stay with their aunt so they wouldn't catch whatever Arthur had.

Just before Dick climbed into the front seat of his pa's truck, Arthur asked Momma if it was okay for him to kiss Dick good-bye. Arthur made it sound like he was worried about spreading his germs. But Dick wondered if maybe it was a revenge kiss; maybe Arthur could tell Dick thought of him as just a little faggy-faced twerp who Momma dressed in girls clothes. Arthur had spent his first few sick days in the room at the top of the stairs, whining for tomato gravy on toast, and it was always Dick who played nursemaid, chasing down cool washrags and carrying dribbling bowls of tomato and bread up the steep wooden staircase. Maybe Arthur knew Dick hated doing these things and only wanted to kiss him so Dick could catch the illness and see how hard it was to be sick.

The little brat was standing there pale faced, arms outstretched, waiting for Dick to offer his cheek, waiting to pucker and show his affection for his older brother. He looked a little too innocent. Dick was certain the little bastard was offering his slimy, disease-infested lips so he could drag Dick down into his quagmire of illness. It wasn't enough that Dick had nearly been crushed by a horse buggy when he was two, or that his bout with pneumonia had almost killed him, or that chronic sinus infections plagued him all year long. Now this little snot-faced shit of a brother wanted to give him the gift of death.

Momma stood waiting. Arthur closed his eyes and puckered. Pa honked the truck's horn and said, "Hurry up, we've got to make the city by noon."

So Dick had no choice. He wanted to say, "No! I don't want his pukey lips on me. Please, Momma. Don't make me." But he couldn't. He was speechless. Arthur smiled, a gaping hole where his two front teeth should have been. Dick stepped forward reluctantly and let the little bugger plant the seeds of death on his left jowl. Then, finally, when the deed was done, he got into the truck with Harold and Pa drove off in a cloud of dust, humping down the road toward the big city with Momma and sick little Arthur in front of the house, waving good-bye.

At Aunt Jane's house, Harold played ghost in the graveyard in the alley with the neighborhood kids. Dick played piano and read about the Teapot Dome Scandal in the city newspapers. Dick's aunt was a piano teacher, and she had given Dick lessons before. He could sight-read and play by ear almost from the start. The aunt told him to sit straight. Proper posture, she said, would keep him from banging the keys so hard. But Dick liked to play the piano hard—until the joints in his fingers and wrists actually began to ache.

When he improvised at the keyboard, Dick could imagine he was in another place. The harder he played, the further away he was able to drift. This was his gift, the aunt had said. But it was also his curse. In these states, when he was drifting off and banging the keys, he played things that were not in the least pleasant or recognizable. He was playing for himself and for the movie he was watching in his head.

One day Dick was pounding out scales when he suddenly launched into one of his extemporaneous keyboard explorations. The aunt was outside watering plants or something, and Harold was gone too. Dick had the house to himself and there was no one to complain about his piano playing. He got lost in the angry noises the chords made. The parlor filled with a sound like truckloads of pianos crashing into one another on a busy highway. Dick smiled and slipped away.

He imagined he was at home, carrying a bowl of steaming oatmeal up to Arthur's sickbed. He slammed out a dissonant minor chord and climbed a stair. The oatmeal sent up a hot puff of steam. Smoke signals. The piano tinkled its response. At the top of the steps Dick crossed the hall into the bedroom where Arthur lay.

A gray light swept the room. Arthur's mouth lay open, his head thrown back, his eyes locked in terror. Arthur's frozen limbs and gray flesh danced a violent jig on the piano keys, and Dick, dropping the bowl of oatmeal, ran down the stairs, out the door, into the field. Running, sweeping his hands across the ivory, he screamed for his pa. Somewhere out there in the stifling heat where withering citrus trees dotted the horizon, Dick's pa was waiting to hear the news of his youngest son's death, waiting to hear the final chord in this chapter of Nixon tragedy, and it was up to Dick to deliver it. He ran and ran, covered every acre, every amelodic chord combination, and still no Pa anywhere. "Pa!" he screamed, "Arthur's dead! Arthur's dead, Pa. Where are you? We need you, Pa. Arthur's dead. He's dead! Oh God, where are you, Pa?" No answer came. But Dick kept running and calling out until finally, Aunt Jane, hearing the furious noise in her parlor, came inside from watering her plants and laid her weathered hands on Dick's shoulders. When she did this he turned around on his stool and buried his face in her apron. She grasped his aching hands and held them tight.

Dick and Harold were asleep on the floor in Aunt Jane's parlor when the lights came on unexpectedly one night. Dick sat up and rubbed his eyes. Pa was standing in front of him with the lamplight shining from behind him. He was casting his thin shadow down on the boys.

Harold said, "Pa, what are you doing here?"

"We're going home, boys," was all Pa said.

They gathered up their things and said good-bye to their aunt, who had come downstairs in her nightgown to see them off. There was a curious, distant look on her face.

Dick and Harold piled into the truck with their pa and headed home. Dick was in the middle of the seat, straddling the gearshift, sandwiched between his older brother and his father.

It was cold and Dick wanted to curl up there on the seat and go back to sleep, but somehow he understood that was not the thing to do. He looked up at his father, who had not said a word since telling the boys they were going home. The truck bounced along noisily, but the three inside were utterly silent. Dick looked at Harold, who was looking at Pa. Then Dick looked back at Pa.

The truck hit a pothole and bounced again. As the truck absorbed the jostling, a small tear jarred itself loose from the corner of Frank Nixon's right eye. It rolled down his cheek. He made no effort to wipe it away.

Dick was sure his father knew he was being watched. Still, Pa let the tear slide its long decline down his stubbled face. Over the next bump in the road, the tear finally dropped off Frank's chin.

The boys did not dare speak. All the way home they were silent, staring straight ahead through the windshield at the long, dark road drawing itself out in front of them.

Dick listened to melodies in his head and thought of how Arthur used to complain about his girly haircut and how at age four, Arthur had once stolen cigarettes for Harold just to show his brothers he was a man even though Momma dressed him like a sissy. Dick remembered, too, Arthur's black eyes and his sailor suit and how his blond hair turned black and curly as he grew out of infancy. But most of all, Dick remembered that toothless kiss Arthur had given him. Dick touched his cheek now as the truck pulled up to the house, and he felt a stinging sensation there that would linger a lifetime.

Dick Nixon
Freshman Composition
Mrs. Worsley
September 22, 1926

My Brother Arthur
An Unforgettable Character

My brother Arthur had black eyes that sparkled with hidden fire and beckoned you on a secret journey which could carry you to Make Believe. My brother Arthur wore a black sailor suit. It was well pressed. His shoestrings were tied in matching bows. His hair was a voluptuous curly brown mess. My brother Arthur died of tuberculosis when he was four years old.

P.S. Mrs. Worsley, this is my description of my brother Arthur. I know you said it should be at least three paragraphs, but this is all I remember about Arthur as I was very young when he died. If you want to know the truth I never liked him very much. He laid in his bed at the top of the stairs moaning all the time. He was very sick. And my mother ran around trying to comfort him all the time. Everyone was very sad when Arthur died, but I didn't really care. As I know this sounds mean, I didn't think I should put any of it in the essay, but since this P.S. is a paragraph long maybe you can see fit to give me credit for two paragraphs out of the three I was supposed to write. Or maybe I could write a different essay on another subject. How about the Teapot Dome Scandal? I know a lot about that.

Funeral

It was a Saturday in September at St. James Episcopal Church on Yakima Avenue in downtown Yakima. It was Ray's wedding day. Ray was nineteen. He was marrying Peggy Wilson, who was sixteen and pregnant.

Ray and Peggy took their vows on the same altar where Ned Paddock's casket had stood the day before. Ned was a friend of Ray's from Yakima High School. They'd graduated together. Ned's casket had been closed. The car wreck left him unrecognizable. Ray was a pallbearer on Friday and a bridegroom on Saturday.

Peggy was at least six or seven weeks along when she stepped up to the altar in her white dress, the organ music fading into a vibrating hush. By now the fetus had a spine. By now it was growing out of its prehistoric aquatic larva stage. By now it had a heart. And the heart was beating. One hundred and forty beats per minute, the doctor had said.

Ray looked at Peggy standing next to him, her face fixed on the minister. He wondered what she'd look like in six or seven months, and he wondered about what kind of mother she'd be. He also wondered what she thought of the name Ned. With Ray's luck the baby would be a girl. But maybe that wasn't so bad. It would give Ray a little practice, which might save him from fucking up his son, if he ever had a son.

The minister said something about *forever* and Ray nodded slightly because he felt it was expected of him. He wanted to squeeze Peggy's hand but she was stiffly holding her bouquet close to her chest. Ray could feel everyone behind him. Family, friends, townspeople. The same people who had been here for Ned's funeral.

Afternoons in the spring Ray and Ned would skip classes and go out to Sportsman's Park to toss rocks across the lake and smoke cigarettes. When their rocks fell short of their mark, ducks would scatter, splashing and rippling the surface of the water. Ray and Ned would laugh and talk about girls they'd like to see naked. Girls they'd like to fuck. They'd make lists of all the girls from their school who they'd like to fuck and then they'd run down the list in order and compare preferences. Peggy was always among the names on Ray's list even though he'd fucked her already. Ned never included Peggy on his list.

When Ray found out Peggy was pregnant, he and Ned stopped going out to Sportsman's. It was expected that Ray would get decent grades and graduate on time so he could work while Peggy finished high school. They couldn't afford for Ray to skip classes anymore, and so in the six weeks before Ned wrapped his Ford around a tree trunk out on Naches Road, Ray hadn't seen much of him at all. And now, standing next to Peggy in his rented tux, he could hardly even remember what Ned's face looked like.

If the baby turned out to be a girl, Ray would tell her to stay away from boys. They can't help themselves, he'd say, but they're all assholes. Trust me, I know. Peggy's parents hated Ray, and who could blame them? But it was done now. The vows, the rings, everything. The baby's heart was beating. Ned was gone. And Ray was getting married.

After the wedding, the minister took Ray and Peggy into his office to have them sign the marriage license. The room smelled like moldy books and sweat. On the wall a pendulum clock swung smugly, going tsk tsk tsk at Ray and Peggy. Sixty times per minute. Not even half a heartbeat.

They signed the papers. Then the minister asked them to sit. He capped his pen and took off his priestly robe. "Raymond," he said, "I don't know what you're looking for in this life. I only know that a life has chosen you. And now you must rise to it. Do you feel you're up to it?"

Ray didn't say anything right away. He shifted in his chair, looked at Peggy, then back at the minister. Was this part of the deal? Was this a required step? The wedding was done and Ray needed a beer. What the fuck was he supposed to say? *Yes, sir, I'm very much up to the challenges this life has dealt me. You can count on me, sir.* What the fuck was that?

The clock tsked. "I'm nineteen years old," Ray finally said. "Yesterday I buried my best friend. Today I got married. On Monday morning I go back to work at the sawmill where my father worked since before I was born. That's all there is. That's it."

No one said anything for a few seconds. They all just looked at each other. But then sixteen-year-old Peggy Wilson, now Mrs. Raymond Carver, stood up and lifted the marriage license off the minister's desk, and as Ray rose to his feet beside her, she said, "Thank you for your concern, sir. But I assure you Ray and I will be just fine. I'm going to finish high school and Ray's going to work. And somehow, some way we're both going to college. I'm going to be a teacher. And Ray is going to be an author. We're getting out of Yakima. You can count on it." With that, she turned and swished out of the minister's office with the marriage license in one hand and her hiked-up dress train in the other.

Ray was left standing at the edge of the minister's desk for a moment, alone there with the minister. The pendulum swung. Somewhere under a damp mound of earth a casket settled into place. The minister stared sternly at Ray, waiting for something.

And then without warning, Ray erupted. It was a hiccupping chuckle at first. Then hyphenated hyena bursts. Eventually, an uncontrollable laughter seized him. He hyperventilated, gagged on his own laughter. The more he laughed, the more stone-faced the minister became. The more stone-faced the minister became, the more Ray laughed. It was as if someone were violently tickling him. He hadn't laughed so hard in years. Maybe he hadn't ever laughed this hard. There was no stopping it. And there was no graceful or mature way out of it. So Ray backed out of the office, waving a surrender at the minister, and he laughed all the way out of the church, all the way to the parking lot.

Out there he found Peggy waiting for him in the passenger seat of the car his father had borrowed for them. His proud pregnant bride was waiting for him, and he was laughing so damn hard that it hurt. When he got behind the wheel of his borrowed car, he was still laughing. With Peggy next to him, he gripped the steering wheel and shut his eyes hard. The laugh tears ran down his face in clear ripples, splashing on the leatherette seat.

According to Aunt Jane

The boy had a gift, there's no doubt about that. He had an ear for it. And the dexterity and passion of a born musician. I'm the one that taught him everything he knew about the piano. My husband gave him violin lessons, but the piano was his real calling.

It was Hannah that made Richard read all the time. Don't get me wrong, she was my sister, God bless her, and a good mother to those boys, but she filled Richard's head full of so much nonsense. Do you know she taught that boy to read before he was even old enough for the infant school? She was teaching him Latin before he could write his own name in English. She even made him memorize Greek myths and famous speeches and Shakespearean sonnets.

I remember one time when he was about four, he got up at the dinner table just after everyone had finished their apple pie, and he recited the whole Gettysburg Address, word for word. Four years old, you ever hear of such a thing? We all clapped and praised the child, of course. But I'll be honest, I thought it was a bit odd to be asking a boy of that age to be doing such things. It would have been one thing if they'd have asked him to play something for us on the upright in the parlor. But what kind of a mother makes her son recite political speeches at the dinner table? Did you know it was her idea to name those boys after the kings of

England? We didn't see eye to eye on some things, Hannah and me.

And as far as Frank was concerned, nobody saw eye to eye with him. He made sure of it. If you said white, he said black. It's no wonder to me Dick turned out like he did. What with Frank making him drink that raw milk all the time, saying that pasteurizing was dirty and evil. None of us were surprised when the boys kept coming down with all those lung ailments. Even Richard got the undulant fever and had a spot on one of his lungs at one time. But Frank refused to believe his cow might be infected. He named the cow Gary Cooper, you know. Now, I'm not saying it was Gary Cooper what made Richard do all the things he did in his lifetime, but if that cow was infected and it was the cause of all that harm that was done to those boys, a lot of hardship could have been avoided, and who knows, Richard might have turned out entirely different.

Frank was so stubborn, especially about those animals he kept. Like that horse of his. Beautiful horse. Loretta Young was her name, I think. Everybody in town said she was the most beautiful horse they'd ever seen. It's because of Loretta that Frank became a Republican, you know. Most people don't know this, but Frank was a staunch Democrat when the boys were young.

When McKinley came to town to campaign, the Republican Campaign Committee in Whittier asked Frank if they could use his horse in the parade. Frank was flattered, of course, but he wouldn't let anybody ride his horse. The boys weren't even allowed to ride her. So he said they could use the horse but only if he rode her. "Fair enough," the campaign people said, "but you gotta promise to keep your opinions to yourself about Mr. McKinley." See, they knew Frank might stir up a ruckus if they didn't keep a leash on him.

But Frank was on his best behavior that day, riding tall on his mare. In fact, he even wore a fine black suit that day. I think it was his funeral-going suit. And they had him ride right behind McKinley's buggy in the parade. So at the end of the parade, the candidate gets out and gives his speech to the townspeople, and then goes around shaking hands. Well, he goes right up to Frank Nixon first before he shakes anybody else's hand and he says, "Mighty fine-looking horse you got there, brother. Thanks for your help with the campaign. Keep up the good work for the party." Well, do you know, from that day on, Frank Nixon was a Republican. And he was the most vocal Republican in town too.

Now, how does a young boy—a bright boy, a gifted boy like Richard—how does he reconcile all this? And that's just the tip of the iceberg. I didn't even tell you about Frank's other habits. Like the time he made a pass at me, his wife's sister, under the table—at Easter, for goodness sakes. But that's not a story for public consumption. I don't want to crucify the man. Still, how does a boy like Richard find his path with these kind of influences? Who knows. But I'm not afraid to say that I wasn't surprised in the least about what became of him when he went to Washington. None of us were—none of us that really knew the family anyway—we weren't surprised at all.

I don't mind telling you I saw he was headed for a fall early on. What with all the problems he had growing up with Frank Nixon as a father and such, not to mention the way his mother was always off on some new adventure to save Harold, the favorite son, in Arizona or some other god-awful place.

Little Dickie would come around, sweet-talking me, saying what a pretty house I had and what a pretty dog, and he'd tell me about how he was real good at mashing potatoes, and how that was his main job in the family. He said he could mash potatoes like nobody's business. It was a little bit spooky the way he talked about it. He used to get this funny look in his eye like he was king of the potato mashers. It was like that was all he had going for him.

One time he told me he didn't wash dishes 'cause doing dishes is a girl's job. So I said to that boy, "Child, doing dishes is the Lord's work just like any other chore, and you got to do it whether you like it or not." Well, he says, "Yes'm," like he learned his lesson, but I asked his momma a few days later if he was doing the dishes, and she said he still wouldn't do them. That just goes to show you what kind of an upbringing that boy had. I'm telling you, if you know the facts, there's no surprise in what came of him.

Dickie Runs

One of Dick's first memories is of running. He's in an all-out sprint alongside a freight train. The tracks run right through Pa's pathetic grove of dying lemon trees. Dick waits for the train. He can hear the whistle in the distance. He jogs slowly at first, gradually picking up speed as the train nears. He has raced this train every day since his first steps, except of course for those months when he was fighting pneumonia and the doctors thought he might have had the same family sickness that took his younger brother Arthur.

Dick was always running someplace—racing trains through lemonless lemon groves, dashing away from a neighbor's vines with hands full of stolen grapes under his shirt, outrunning tumbleweed and rattlers—forever running, conditioning himself. Wiping out the traces of pneumonic tissue in his little lungs.

They say he was the family's loudest crier, born premature during a rare California cold snap that would've froze the nipples off a corpse. Screamed like a savage, they say, just to let everybody know, sickly or not, weren't no TB going to catch up with him.

Years later, when the disease skipped over Dick and took hold of his older brother Harold, Dick kept running. There along the tracks, neck and neck with a grain car, he decided someday he'd be a train conductor and make them rails smoke with his speed. Someday trains would move at the speed of sound, and Dick would be at the controls, leaving behind his father's dusty failures and his pathetic brothers who didn't have the balls to fight their weak-lunged fate.

Harold and that zitty little brat Glenda from down the road— they always sat out there beyond the tracks, hiding behind Pa's brittle citrus branches, out there in Pa's grove, playing show-and-tell. All the while, Harold was on the TB express to Quaker hell, the devil lurking in his pus-filled lungs, waiting for the right moment to strike.

Harold says, "Go get us some lemonade, Dickie boy. I bet you can't get back before I count a hundred." Dickie knows why Harold wants to be alone with that little turd Glenda. Harold probably thinks Dickie is too young to understand this.

Dickie runs for the lemonade. Not because Harold told him to. Not because anybody actually wants lemonade. No, Dickie runs because he likes to run and because he's good at it and because he knows weakly old Harold will collapse in a spit-pool of his own blood one day, hacking up a lung in between a row of Pa's dying twigs. Harold will be on his knees, looking up at Glenda one minute, and the next he'll be face flat in manure, praying for forgiveness. Glenda will shriek and old Harold will wheeze his last good-bye to Yorba Linda. And while all this is happening, young innocent Dick Nixon will be sprinting through the dry field, sucking the dusty air deep through flaring nostrils.

Dick fills his spongy lungs, expels, and then fills again. The trees rustle but he can't even hear them. He's trampling through irrigation ditches, sidestepping dung piles, leaning this way and that. He can hear Harold counting to one hundred in the distance, Glenda giggling. There's nothing in Dick's way but air. He'll breathe it all in, fill himself with all of California's dry oxygen, swallow the atmosphere whole.

In one huge breath, Dick bursts through the kitchen door.

"Lemonade, Momma," he calls. "Harold wants lemonade."

"The poor dear," Momma says. "He must be parched. Why

does he stay out there in this heat? I've told him a hundred times it's no good for his condition."

Dick wants to say, Fuck him, Momma. Your precious Harold is going to be buried alongside your precious Arthur before long. He's lost to you, Momma. The old scar-lunged wheezer is out there at this very moment praying for a sneak peek at little Glenda Newcomb's crotch. There's nothing but the devil in Harold now, Momma!

But Dickie is Momma's good dog, and so he bites his little Quaker tongue and just says, "The lemonade, Momma. Hurry!"

The screen door slams behind Dick as he sprints for the finish with sloshing glass pitcher in hand. Back through ditch and manure obstacles, he dodges, listening for Harold's voice, listening for the countdown to victory. A race with Satan. A race with the family disease.

"Ninety-seven, ninety-eight, ninety-nine," Harold calls.

Dickie lunges forward, splashing sour yellow on Glenda's smart summer dress. It's been a long season of dry citrus and throaty family rasps, and never once has Harold reached one hundred before young Richard finished running.

The Family Name

Harold said, "Go ahead. I double dare you, Dickie."

Dick thought about it. Here it was, his birthday, and him in his best Sunday knickers. If he got them dirty, Momma would hide in her closet all night, whimpering prayers, pleas for her son's salvation. And there'd be no telling what Pa would do. Dick clearly had to weigh the consequences.

Harold egged on: "Come on, pimple butt. What are you waiting for? Jump."

Harold turned to Cousin Clifford and Maribelle. "I told you he's afraid of water. Always has been, ever since he was just a wee little Dickie. Used to sit by the side of that tree over there and slobber on himself—'Momma, don't make me go in the water, there's slimies in there.'"

"Not true," Dick managed, but it was true and everyone knew it. "Anyway, that was a long time ago, you idiot head. I was just a baby practically. I'm not afraid anymore."

"Show us then," said Harold with a cough. "Show us how you swim in the muck, Dick-Boy."

"Harold, if he doesn't want to," said Maribelle.

Dick wanted to say, Harold's a dumb dork-face with throw-up in his lungs. I hope Harold coughs so hard, he chokes and dies and God sends him straight to hell.

Harold laid it on his little brother: "You're a chicken. He's a chicken. Gobble gobble waddle waddle little chicken-neck. Where's Pa's hatchet? Maybe I oughta chop your big dumb head off right now and put you out of our misery."

"Come on, Harold," said Cousin Clifford, "leave him alone. It's his birthday. Besides, we should all be getting back to the party, before we get hollered at. We been gone a long while."

"Clifford my boy, do what you want, but I'm staying out here until Dickie baptizes himself in this here pond. Even if I have to sit under that tree the rest of the season and into the deep winter. I ain't letting this cootie get off easy."

"Fine, you jerk face," said Dick. And with that he plugged his nose with fingers and plunged himself into the green water, fully clothed in his Sunday best.

Horrible slime plants grabbed Dick's ankles and pulled him down. Demon muck filled his ears. The filth tugged at him. He flailed and splashed, bobbed to the surface, swallowing mouthfuls of the infested water. He heard laughter. Harold's laughter—big and hoarse, a coughing fit of laughter, laughing so hard that by now he had hacked up a mouthful of his bloody tuberculous phlegm. Cousin Clifford and Maribelle would be slapping Harold on the back, to save him from drowning in his own mucus.

The wiggling weeds grabbed hold of Dick again. He shut his eyes tight, gasped for air, and was sucked down again and again. Finally he stopped fighting it—lost the will. As he sank to the bottom, the water spoke to him in wavy rhythms. The pond was an uninfected lung, breathing, and Dick was just a molecule of air floating about, waiting to be expelled.

On the bottom of Miller's pond, Dick opened his eyes and saw the water life clinging to his knickers. He knew then why Harold had done this to him. He knew then what it would mean to be the only surviving Nixon boy, the only one who would not be struck down by lungs full of human algae. He knew the burden of living that lay ahead.

Eventually, the air Richard kept hidden in his pink little lungs carried him to the surface again. He floated upward like a cottonwood seed on a breezy summer's day. When Dick bobbed back to the surface and looked about, he saw Harold sitting on the side of the pond, still coughing. In the distance, Cousin Clifford and Maribelle were running to the house for help.

Harold spotted Dickie floating in the muck. His coughing ceased at once. Harold smiled at Dick, waved a congratulations, and gave him the thumbs-up. Dick smiled too and waved back. He floated on his back casually despite the green slop all around him. Harold began laughing a gentle wheezing laugh. Dick swam toward shore.

By then Cousin Clifford and Maribelle were running back to the pond with Pa trailing behind them, his eyes so big you could feel them vibrating in their sockets. Dick was climbing out of the water, hunks of water fungus dangling from every crevice of his lumpy little body.

"You cretins," bellowed Pa. "You fowl little monkey cretins. I'll tan you both, and skin you alive. You mucky little fleabags. What in God's tarnation in the hell is wrong with you?" Pa's thundering footsteps landed him like God's son himself—the end of the world—right there on the shore of that hideous little pond.

Harold was rising from his place on a rock, hunched and still breathing heavy from his fit. Richard was rising out of the shallow end like some evil lagoon creature.

That's when Pa, being the kind of man that he was, grabbed them both by the scruffs of their necks with his big bear claws and said, "You like water? Have some more." And with that, he flung them both deep into the heart of the pond and cackled his pointy Frank Nixon laugh.

Sheep Dip

Ray was riding in a car with his older brother, his only brother, Eddie. They had no particular destination. They had considered fishing but weren't in the mood. They were driving just to feel the road rush under them as they headed nowhere.

Eddie was talking about how his wife wanted to have their cat neutered and about a movie he had seen recently. Ray tried to say something of consequence, tried to relate his brother's movie experience to a book he'd been reading. But Eddie hadn't read a book since high school, except maybe a law-scam thriller or two. Ray said, "Maybe your cat would be better off with functioning genitals. I hear they get fat and lazy when you get them fixed." Eddie laughed and said something about needing to replace a screen door on his back porch at home.

The road was moving fast and gray beneath them. Eddie steadied a pint of Sheep Dip on the steering wheel and took a long drink. He passed Ray the bottle. It was warm from being between Eddie's legs. Ray drank from the bottle—this was in the days when he was still doing that—then recapped the bottle, leaned back, and watched as the corn fields rushed past. Another flat mid-western state. Feed corn and soybean stretching to the horizon. Occasionally, a silo or steeple interrupted the moving canvas outside the car window.

This little trip was Eddie's idea. "I'll tell the wife we're going for a ride," he had said. "We'll just go. You and me," he'd said. A summit, a reunion. What choice did Ray have? So they bought a couple pints and left. Just like that.

When they were kids, Eddie used to call Ray "Jew Boy," and he said he was embarrassed for his friends to know he and Ray were related. Neither one of them even knew what a Jew was in those days, but it sounded like a bad thing, like cooties. In junior year, when Ray's batting average plummeted below .150, he quit the baseball team and Eddie started calling him Fag-Wham.

After Eddie graduated high school he married a woman named Lena who flushed her toothbrushes down the toilet when she was done with them. Ray got an English degree and an editing job with a textbook company. He wrote poems in his spare time, but he was trying to raise a kid and keep his own wife happy. Eddie got a job tending bar.

They drove from one prairie town to the next, stopping only for gasoline and corn nuts at the local Sunway stations. Beyond talk of feline genitalia, there wasn't anything to say, but the silence between them was pregnant with the kind of expectant energy that always exists between two men who share the same mother and father. Ray imagined that they passed the bottle of Sheep Dip back and forth across the vinyl expanse of car seat like words of an unspeakable sentence they were collaborating on and planning to diagram later—too many passive verbs and weak-kneed modifiers, a rambling fragment of exquisite proportions, like a sentence uttered by the feeble lips of Yogi Berra. They punctuated only when their hands touched accidentally. They exchanged a glance over the bottle of Sheep Dip, and Ray wondered if there was any such thing as accident. If he ever wrote a poem about this moment, he decided, that's what he would call it—"Accident."

By the time they were half-way through their second pint, Ray had forgotten the gray asphalt that brought them to this summit meeting. The car seemed to stand still. It was the corn which was in motion, whizzing by them in a hurry to turn yellow before the harvest.

Eddie laughed at something Ray said which was not intended to be funny. Eddie's laugh was a hearty one—hearty but forced, like he wanted to laugh harder than he was able. Ray laughed with him. He figured he owed Eddie that much at least. When Eddie gets drunk, he looks a lot like our father, Ray thought. One eye droops and there's something dangerous in his smile. By the time they reached the DeKalb county line, both of them were pretty well gassed up.

Eddie said out of nowhere in typical Eddie fashion, "You know why women don't like to suck cock?"

Ray threw up his heavy drunken hands.

Eddie slurred, "Because they're afraid of the snake's power, little brother. They know—one false move, and it's choke city." He let go of the steering wheel and grabbed his throat as if to choke himself, eyes bugging out and tongue waggling.

Somewhere in his sober self Ray was completely repulsed by his brother, but at that moment, with the speedometer approaching ninety and the corn parting around them like the Red Sea and the Sheep Dip pulsing through him, Ray saw only wisdom. The choking power of the penis. That was what his brother knew. That was all Eddie could pass on to Ray.

Ray laughed and heard himself say something he'd heard in a beer commercial once: "It don't get no better than this." Ray wondered how this sentence would look diagrammed. And he wondered why he didn't say things like this more often. Ray handed Eddie the Sheep Dip and closed his eyes again. He listened to the steady hum of the tires and decided he'd recline his passenger seat and just let Eddie drive them to China and back—Eddie at the wheel chewing his Doublemint, tapping his left foot in time to the dotted white lines flying past, Eddie laughing that laugh of his, infecting Ray with it. In fact, Ray decided, it would be all right with him if he died right there and then.

But Ray knew it was all too good to be true. Any minute, they'd blow a tire and spin out into a ditch. Or maybe they'd stop to pick up a hitchhiker who'd talk their ears off about politics and baseball. Or maybe the car would simply veer off into the corn, and Eddie would drive them straight to hell. Worse yet, Eddie might just stop the car, nudge Ray out of his beautiful coma, and say, "We're home, little brother."

Dick & Ray & Me

Nixon's got that look in his eye—the one he gets when his metal detector starts beeping and he thinks he's on to a big find. Beady and shifty. He licks his lips.

Carver rolls another maggot under his tongue. He's keeping them warm, just as his old man taught him. Or maybe it wasn't his dad who taught him that. Maybe that's just something he put in a poem once and now, all these years later, it seems like it really happened that way. In any case, the maggots are squirming around in there, trying to get loose. But Carver has got them tongue locked.

I'm at the stern end, trying to bait a fly or fly a hook or whatever the hell they call it. I'm using rubber bait with these feathery ends and an orange bobber I got on special at Sportmart just for this trip.

At first, no one says much. There's scaly game to hunt. Nixon's out for blood. No one's going to tell him humans came from aquatic amoebae. This is man against fish. No remorse. Dick wants to snag the gilled bastards with a sharp snatch and a whip of his brand new Zebco. Carver is meticulous. His rod is the last in the water. He sits and waits, staring off into the trees. I'm tugging at my line, waiting for something to happen. Nixon casts and reels, casts and reels. He can't sit still. He's stirring our waters, but Carver says nothing. In fact, when I look closely, I could swear

Ray's lips are moving in silent prayer. Maybe he's praying we don't catch anything. Maybe he's praying Nixon falls out of the boat. Maybe he's praying I stop staring at him. Or maybe he's just singing to himself, some little ballad written before my time.

Out of nowhere Nixon says, "I'll call it Penisaurus rex." Carver's onto him in no time. No explanation needed. It's as if the conversation started years ago and they're just picking up where they left off. Carver says, "Does the wife call it Rex? For short?"

"She calls it by its full name, you fuck," says Nixon, "because it ain't never short when she's around. In fact, it ain't never short. Period."

"So you conquered that impotence problem, eh?" Carver wants to know.

"Listen, doughboy, it ain't real impotence unless it happens all the time. It's just that woman of mine can't get enough of me, that's the problem. But then, who could blame her?"

"Even since you gained your postpresidential forty?"

"Are you kidding? Now she's got more of me to crave."

Finally, I join in. Bravely, I manage, "Gosh, I wish I had your problems, Dick. My F.O.I. is way down."

"What's F.O.I.?" Carver asks.

"Frequency of intercourse, you doofus," Nixon informs, casting his line emphatically.

"What's your F.O.I.?" I ask Ray.

"Oh, about once a week, at best. Depending."

"That's about what I'm up against too," I say. Then I ask him how he can stand it.

Ray's reaching in his tackle box for something. He says, "Beth subscribes to the Victoria's Secret catalog. I keep myself entertained when necessary. If you know what I mean."

I know exactly what he means, but I don't let on. Instead, I ask, "What's up with women's appetites anyway?"

Carver says, "What appetites?"

"That's exactly what I mean," I say.

Nixon reels his line in and offers his philosophy. "All women are lesbians," he says.

That sort of stifles us for a minute. We're thinking about it. Or at least I am. I can't tell what Ray is thinking until he says, "Beth had a *Cosmo* laying around the house last week, so I pick it up and start flipping through it, you know. Anyway, I read in there that lots of women don't have orgasms at all. That would slow anybody's appetite, I suppose."

"Nothing would slow Pat's appetite. But then, she's fucking the president of the United States of America."

"Ex-president," Carver says. And then he says, "In that *Cosmo* article, it said that nonorgasmic women need to explore their own bodies and find out what pleases them."

"Shit," says Nixon. "Men have known that for years. That's why we *always* come."

"Only if we can get it up first," Carver adds. "*Cosmo* says the best place for a woman to do it is in the bathtub so she doesn't feel dirty and guilty about doing it."

"What's to feel guilty about?" Nixon wants to know. "Say, speaking of baths," he says, "I took such a mean shit this morning that I had to take a freaking bath right afterward just to get myself clean." Dick shifts his weight and rocks the boat a bit. "That ever happen to you?" he asks Ray.

"Used to," Carver says. "Every Sunday morning when I had the beer shits."

I want to contribute so I tell them about my brother-in-law who used to be in the army and about how in the army, they only give you one sheet of paper towel a day to wipe your ass with.

Nixon giggles. He says, "You're making that up.

"No. I swear it's the truth," I say.

"Your brother-in-law is full of shit. I was the fucking commander in chief of the fucking armed services. Don't you think I'd know if something like that was going on?"

Carver says, "Well, I think they should have bidets in the army. Think how much tax money we'd save on paper costs."

"I remember the first time I saw one of them bidet things,"

Nixon says. "I didn't know what the hell it was. I just figured it was some kind of weird woman thing I shouldn't be messing with. You know, I think I'd get a boner if I sat on one of them things."

"Dig that anal stimulation, eh, Richard?" Carver asks.

"What can I say?" Nixon says. "It's as close as I come to understanding women."

I have a story to tell. And while I'm reasonably certain Nixon will appreciate it, I can't be sure Carver will be interested, but it's all I have to offer. I tell them about the time I was a kid at the beach with my day camp troop, and I had to take a turd, but I was too scared and embarrassed to ask if I could go to the john, so I shit in my swim trunks in the lake, but then I was afraid to release the turd from my suit because I thought it would float up to the top of the water and follow me around and I wouldn't be able to swim away fast enough and everyone would know the turd was mine. So I kept it in my trunks all day, and later, when they took us to the changing rooms, I took my trunks off real careful and kept the turd in there, thinking I could drop it on the ground when nobody was looking. But then, next thing I know, we're getting on the bus to go home, and so I thought maybe I'd drop in on the ground outside the bus before I got on, but there were too many people around, so I had to get on the bus with the turd still in my swim trunks, and I thought maybe if nobody sat near me I could just keep the turd in there till I got home, but of course some kid sat next to me and I could smell the turd heating up in the palm of my hand so I had to get rid of it. So when the kid sitting next to me turned his head for a second, I unleashed that turd and let it roll onto the floor. I was hoping to boot it away from me, but he turned around too fast, so I played dumb and said, "Oh my God look at that, it's a turd." The kid just looked at me real funny like he could see right through me, but he didn't say anything. He just sat there staring. We watched the turd roll back and forth all the way home. At every stoplight it rolled forward, and every time the driver hit the gas it rolled back. We'd lift our feet so it wouldn't hit us. The kid next to me watched the turd but didn't talk to me. After a while, I looked out the window and tried to pretend the turd wasn't even there.

The whole time I'm telling the story, Nixon is squirming with delight, slapping his knee from time to time. Casting and reeling all the while.

Carver just stares off. I can't read him. But when I'm done, he says, "That's a hell of a story." Nixon's wiping laugh tears from the corner of his beady eyes. Carver doesn't say anything else. He reels in his line for the first time. He checks his bait, pulls a fresh maggot from between his gums.

After he gets the hook baited, Carver climbs out of the boat and wades in up to his hips. The water rushes up around him. He's in past his balls, but he doesn't make a fuss. Finally he says, "My old man made me wipe my ass with his snotty handkerchief once."

"Why the hell did he do that?" Nixon wants to know.

"We were at the Moose lodge. There was no toilet paper. So he gave me his snot-rag and said, 'Here. Use this, son.' " He casts his line. The bobber lands with a gentle slap and the hook sinks below, waiting. "I remember when I flushed the old man's hand-kerchief, I felt so guilty," Carver says. "I was worried about what the old drunk would do if he had to blow his nose."

The sun is full up now. The air is warming. It's doubtful we're going to catch anything. Carver wades out a little further. A trout jumps in the distance, laughing at us. Nixon keeps casting, against the odds—oblivious.

I offer this: "I used to get my ass kicked in junior high all the time."

Nobody responds at first. Then Nixon says, "I was a weakly little fuck when I was in school. Tattletale too. Guess I deserved to get my ass kicked. These shithead varsity football players used to chase me home after school. I'd have to plan a different escape route every day. One time they held me down and let cheerleaders take turns punching me."

"Did you ever tell your parents about it?" I ask him.

"Are you kidding? Frank Nixon would have kicked my ass if

I told him I was getting my ass kicked. I once made the mistake of telling him I wanted to be a concert pianist when I grew up, and he hit me so hard I thought he busted my eardrum."

"Fathers," Carver says. And that pretty much says it all.

I'm wondering what the fish would add to this conversation if they could speak. I'm wondering what role fish fathers play after they've planted their seed. Nixon has finally stopped fly-casting, but only for a moment. He rubs the back of his hairy neck, shakes his jowls, and shifts his weight. He resumes casting. I wonder if he's ever actually caught a fish. I think of Carver's story about the fishermen. The one where they find the dead woman floating in the water. What would we do, the three of us, if we found a woman facedown along the shoreline?

Carver reels in his line and wades back to the boat. He climbs in. He's soaking wet. He tells us a story about his father's father. The guy had Parkinson's or Hodgkin's. Carver can't remember which. Anyway, Carver's father's father went into an icy lake one November with nothing but a bottle of whiskey to keep him company. It was the last time anybody ever saw the old bastard.

Nixon's old man was a gun freak. Shot his rifle into the coal bin in the cellar at night, just for fun.

I tell them my great-great-grandfather owned a tavern once, and these guys were picking on his brother, so he reached under the bar, pulled out a shotgun, and blew them both to smithereens. Then I tell them my grandpa on my mother's side was a real mild-mannered guy—the bowtie type. He even tended flowers out in back of his house. Even cooked for my grandma when she took ill.

Nixon says, "That's why your F.O.I. is down, you pud whacker. You got florist blood pumping through that little penis of yours." He laughs his tight, pointy-nosed laugh.

It's getting on toward midday. I reel my line in and set the rod down in the boat. I'm tired of fishing. I'm tired of talking. I'd like to lie back in the boat, lean up against Ray's back, put my feet up on Dick. I'd like to just let the sun soak in and listen to them talk all day.

I have no use for fish. But that's why we're here. So I decide to change bait. Ray spits a maggot into my hand. I hook it on the end of my line and cast out as I've watched Dick do all morning. Then I just let my line sit. None of us is going to catch a damn thing. Still, here I am, fishing with Dick and Ray.

Nixon wants to hook the scaly bastards, cut them open, watch them bleed—rise to the challenge. Ray, he's happy just to keep the maggots warm and tell stories about his old man. And me? I'm just along for the ride. Taking stock. Listening. Trying to learn something. Making use.

Good Dog

My dear Master,

I am writing to say hello to you and Harold in Arizona. I hope the fresh air is helping Harold's lungs feel better. I hope you are well. Today I went on a fishing trip with some boys. They were mean and they made fun of me. When we were walking, one boy whose name is George tripped me and I fell. The other boy made fun of me I got dirty. Jimmy that's the other boy he tried to kick dirt on me. I did a bad thing then. I grabbed George by the ankles and pulled him down to the ground. I wrestled him down and got on top of him and bit him in the arm. He kicked and screamed and I bit harder and he started bleeding and the blood was in my mouth and I spit it out and bit him again in another spot until he bled some more and I chewed up a piece of his skin and spit it in his face. I know you will be angry with me so I got up and started running and I was so scared I guess I was swinging my arms around and I hit a wasp hive with my paw and got stung by swarms of bees and they bit my face and my eyes and now my eyelids are so swollen up I can hardly see this paper in front of me. I wish you would come home right now. I am sorry about Harold and I am sorry I bit that boy George.

Your good Dog,

Richard

Salvation

"The invitation to lean on the Lord is for the weak and lazy," said Frank Nixon. It was his job to teach Sunday school at the Whittier Friends Church. His job to instill moral courage into the minds of Whittier's youth. His job to help them see the evil in their midst. He also had a personal mission to spice up the Quaker ways a little, teach the children that the ways of God didn't always have to be so dull, so predictably peaceful.

"In the sweat of thy face, shalt thou eat bread," Frank said.

A pug-faced boy in the front wiggled in his chair. Frank fell upon the boy with the weight of salvation. "Boy, don't you know it's God's will to test your courage? Who do you think you are, Warren G. Harding?" The boy, wide-eyed, turned white. A five-year-old ghost.

The child's name was Henry. His parents owed money to the Nixon Grocery. Frank had been carrying them on credit for months, but somehow in church they managed to make a public display of their generous donations. Henry was under the spell of his parents' evil ways, and it was up to Frank to save the boy. He boomed, "God knows no bounds, my boy. If you think you can squirm in that chair unnoticed, you are thumbing that little pug nose of yours at the Almighty. Every day is a test, my son. Every moment of every day is a challenge to your moral courage. Every second is a lesson to be learned. You think God doesn't see you? You think I don't see you? There's nowhere to hide, boy."

Henry sat up straight, but his head retreated into his neck in a turtlelike gesture of fear. The other boys, including Frank's own sons, rejoiced privately at Henry's reprimand. This was why they all liked Mr. Nixon so much. This was why his Sunday school class always overflowed, standing room only.

Frank especially liked to teach the unruly boys. He knew he could cure them, prepare them for the Second Coming. In time every last boy in that room would know that this life was not his own, and that this life was not the only one he'd live. The unruly boys, boys like his own Harold, these were the ones who had the most to offer to themselves and to the world because there was fire in these boys. Real flames that could be tamed and channeled. He himself had been like these boys at one time. Still like them really, but now he knew the difference between using the fire to fight God's battle and using it to wage war for the Dark One. That's what he would teach these young pups. Discipline and the proper timing of explosion.

One minute they'd be sitting straight and silent; memorizing the word of the Lord. The next, they were chanting and hollering and screaming God's message. No other Sunday school teacher let them scream in class.

"When I was a younger man," said Frank, "I owned a farm in Yorba Linda. My boys were all born there," he said, nodding at Dick and Harold in the front row. "One of my boys even died there. And then my crops died. They said I should have fertilized more, but I knew if God meant for those crops to grow, they'd grow with or without. They said I was cheap, but I was allowing God's will to show me the way. Well, my crops failed, boys. But do you think I squirmed and cried, and said, 'Why hast thou forsaken me?' I did not. Because I knew God's will had been done. So I sold that land. And you know what happened then, my boys?"

They had heard the story before, but they pretended not to know.

"I'll tell you what happened," said Frank. "The men who bought my land struck oil on it. That's right. Oil. And now they're stinking rich, without a care in the world." He paused for a moment to let this sink in, then asked, "What color is oil, boys?"

The boys cried out on command, "Oil is black!"

"That's right, and what does blackness represent?"

"Black is evil!" they yelled in unison.

"So what is oil then?!"

"Oil is evil!" cried the boys. "Oil is evil," they chanted. "Oil is evil. Oil is evil. Oil is evil." They yelled until Frank Nixon raised a hand to silence them.

"So you see, boys. If I had cried about my woes, if I had fidgeted in my seat when God was trying to teach me a lesson, I might have struck oil, and then I'd be living with the devil coursing through my veins. God saved me from that possessed land and sent me to Whittier. Here to this church and you boys, so that I could continue to raise my sons and spread His message to you foul little monkeys." Frank's gaze bored a hole through little Henry.

Henry stood at the side of his desk, staring at his feet, his lower lip puffed out. He spoke the words he'd been taught to speak in these instances: "Mr. Nixon, sir, I am sorry for my rude misconduct. I am sorry I let the evil in my heart control me. I will try harder to fight it in the future." Having said this, Henry stood motionless at the side of his desk. Frank stepped toward him, laid a hand on his right shoulder, and told the boy to be seated.

"Vengeance is mine sayeth the Lord!" howled Frank.

And the boys howled back, "Vengeance is mine!"

At the end of their time together that Sunday, Frank gave the boys their usual assignment. He said, "Boys, this week I want each of you to ask your parents to stop by my store and pick up a newspaper for you. I want you to read the newspaper from cover to cover. The devil is at work all around you. And if you love your God and your country, you will find the evil around you and wipe it out. I want you to search for the devil's work in our community and in other communities across the country. There is scandalous behavior which we must stamp out together."

"Remember when I told you about my days as a streetcar man?" asked Frank.

The boys nodded.

"Remember how I got frostbite in my toes?"

Again they nodded.

"Remember how I fought the men in charge so that streetcar work would be safe for those that came after me?"

The boys remembered vividly. The frozen toes and the battle for justice. This was always one of their favorite stories. They liked the idea of fighting something. Every last one of them. Even little Henry. But especially the unruly boys. They were itching for a fight. And Frank promised them one every week.

"This is God's ultimate lesson," Frank said. "We must make our evil hearts work for us, not against us." He paused to make sure they understood. Satisfied, he said, "Next week we will continue our discussion of the corruption all around us. Henry, I'll expect you to review all the major events of the upcoming week for us."

"Yes, sir," said Henry.

"You boys run along now," said Frank. "And give my best to your parents."

"Thank you, Mr. Nixon," the boys all said.

When the room cleared out, Frank Nixon gathered up his Bible and his newspaper clippings. Then he took Dick and Harold home, where together they would begin another week of God's work, another week in search of salvation.

Dick held his father's hand all the way home while Harold skipped ahead of them, oblivious of everything. Dick felt the calluses on his father's hand and struggled to keep up with Frank's marching stride. God's holy light filled Frank Nixon's eyes as he and his boys headed for home.

Leg

The worst job Ray ever had was working in the county morgue. They needed the money. It was a job. There weren't a lot of riches to be made in the poetry business. Ray did what he had to do.

Peggy was waiting tables at this shitty little diner, and when she got home, Ray would go down to the morgue. He was on the night crew. Hell, he *was* the night crew. Mostly he cleaned up and just kept an eye on things—made sure none of the cadavers got up and walked away. The job wasn't hard. In fact, he usually got a little writing time in after the place was swept, mopped, and sanitized. He even wrote a poem once about the autopsy room.

Ray's poem was about this one particular night when he saw something that really knocked him back a step or two. You were always seeing things in the autopsy room. Sometimes you could tell yourself you had dreamed it when you nodded off on the sofa in the staff lounge. But sometimes there was no way you could shake the thing you had seen. This was one of those nights.

It was a Wednesday. If it had been a Thursday or Friday it would have been easier to swallow because he'd have had the weekend to look forward to. But from a Wednesday perspective, the weekend's still too damn far away to be a pacifier. When something bad happens at work on a Wednesday, all you can think about is whether or not you can afford to quit. This was definitely a Wednesday.

As far as the weather or time of year, it's impossible to say. Being inside the morgue is like being in a vault or a cave or your own damn tomb. You're so out of touch when you're in that place, what with all the stainless steel tables and white cinder block walls and buzzing fluorescent lights. Even the music over the speaker system sounded synthetic.

It was Wednesday and it was night and Ray was mopping the floor in the autopsy room. If the story ended there it would be depressing enough all by itself. But naturally, there's more to it.

Sometimes the coroners quit early on Wednesday, it being a golf day. And when they did this, they often left in a hurry. If you cleaned the autopsy room every night, it was inevitable that eventually you'd come across something that the coroners left lying out in the open—something that should have been in a bucket of fluid or behind a steel refrigerator door.

One time Ray came across a little baby. A purple green baby, stiff as granite. It was just lying there on the table with its feet up in the air and its mouth open. Another time the coroners left a dead guy laying out on the table. They had cut him open from throat to groin and scooped out his innards like he was a goddamn turkey or something. The guy's giblets had been flopped into a silver pan, and that was lying out still too. The bloody mess was dripping over the edge of the pan, making a little puddle on the counter.

He sat in the head coroner's office that night and wrote a poem about all the ways in which his life might have been different— all the other jobs he could have done. He imagined himself a famous poet, a musician, a preacher, a farmer, a politician, anything but a guy who cleans the autopsy room.

But this one particular Wednesday was the Wednesday to beat all Wednesdays. He had cleaned almost the entire room before he even saw it. His bucket of Clorox and water was already a gray-green red color, and his mop needed to be wrung. He was dragging a rag across the side of the table in the center of the room.

There was a sheet over the bottom half of the table. He could have left well enough alone. He knew better by now. Curiosity killed the cat, and all of that. But he couldn't help himself. So he reached the stiff edge of the fabric and peeled it back.

The leg was pale and severed just below the hip. That's all there was. It was the kind of leg a boy fantasizes about when he first discovers how to give himself pleasure. The arch of the foot curved with a gentle, innocent wrinkle from heel to big toe. The calf was well-defined, athletic even, and smooth looking—freshly shaven. Slightly bent at the girlish knee, the leg invited Ray to its thigh. It was the thigh of a beautiful, wholesome Catholic woman or a two-bit junkie whore. No way to tell.

Men spend their whole lives looking for a leg like that, but the last place you expect to find one is on an autopsy table in a morgue, all by itself, unattached to anything. Ray was lost somewhere between day and night, summer and winter, life and death, success and failure, the present and the future, heaven and hell, arousal and disgust. He wished there were a name for what he was feeling, but he was sure no one had ever felt this before him, and he was relatively certain no one would feel it after him. There would never be a word for it. He decided that was probably for the best and put the sheet back over the leg.

When he got home, Ray went straight to bed. Peggy was still sleeping. She had another hour or two before the alarm clock would go off. Ray turned to face the wall, pulled the sheets up around himself, and shivered. Peggy rolled over then and draped her arm over him, an unintentional sign of affection she would deny by sunrise. She pressed herself up against Ray and slid her knee between his legs. Her warm thigh lingered against him for a minute. Just long enough to make him shiver again. Then Peggy groaned, rolled over again, pulled some of his sheets away from him, and pressed her bony ass up against his.

Ray lay awake until the alarm went off and Peggy got up for work. He thought about the first man and the first woman to inhabit the planet. He wondered what ever gave them the idea to have sex. He wondered if they were repulsed by it but did it out of some instinctive awareness of necessity. He wondered if they told themselves it was fun so that one day they might overcome their hatred of the act. He wondered specifically about the woman and why she submitted to it.

Ray remembered the first time he had seen ducks mating when he was a boy out hiking with his father. One male stood on the back of the female while two others bit her neck and held her head down to the ground so the fourth male could mount her from behind. Ray remembered chasing the males away from the female when he saw it happening because he thought they were attacking her. His father had laughed at him for trying to save the female duck. That was the first time his father told him about sex. It was lesson number one. The other lessons came on the playground from Tommy Pielin's cousin who said, "The guy puts his dick in there and pees, man. But she's gotta be bleeding first or it don't work."

After Peggy took her shower, she came back into the room and got dressed while Ray pretended to sleep. She wiggled into her underwear and then the panty hose and a satiny slip. When she left, she slammed the front door a little too hard, just as she did every day.

Finally, after she was gone, Ray drifted off to sleep. He slept the rest of the day and then got up, ate an egg salad sandwich and went back to the autopsy room to clean up as he would every day for four more years.

According to Gordon

Living down the road from the Nixon family, I had plenty of opportunity to observe the boy as he grew into a man. He used to say he wanted to be a farmer when he grew up.

I have a theory that when a boy needs love and can't find it in his own immediate family because of hardships that claim all the family's attention, he begins to look for it in other places. For Dick, the search might have rested with a family pet or an especially attentive teacher or, who knows, maybe even an artist or a poet he admired. But the truth of the matter is Dick found the love he was looking for when he discovered the beautiful strength and responsiveness of the Nixon family's farm equipment. He started small with shovels and rakes. Eventually, he graduated to larger, more powerful equipment. And while this may seem impossible to imagine, I happen to know that at one point during his difficult youth, Dick fell profoundly in love with a one-bottom plow. Later, when he entered his adolescent stages, it was a John Deere tractor that threw him for a willie of a loop.

It was a big green John Deere with a backhoe attachment. You can ask anyone around here. The folks that were here in those days know all about it. The family tried to keep it a secret of course, but something like that is pretty hard to keep under wraps for very long.

Dick would polish and scrub that old tractor until well past dusk every night. He'd be out there in the twilight humming a tune to his tractor, something that sounded vaguely like "Is You Is or Is You Ain't My Baby?" I can still picture Hannah sitting in her rocking chair on the porch, knitting something pink, and Frank reading the newspaper, muttering something to himself while Dick scrubbed and hummed. He'd hum his little tune over and over like a lullaby, and the tractor would gleam and sparkle in response to his humming.

Now the story goes that one August morning Hannah discovered some of her underwear and stockings and things missing from one of her drawers. She questioned Frank and the boys, but none of them seemed to know anything about it. She couldn't imagine where her things might have disappeared to, but she put it out of her head because she had greater concerns on her mind.

Well supposedly, the very next day all of the missing things magically reappeared on her dresser in a neatly stacked pile. She picked up her slip on top of the pile, and held the satin material between her fingers. She noticed a stain. She brought the fabric to her nose. The smells of hay, motor oil, and red wine rose up to meet her.

Hannah is said to have walked to the window and looked out to the fields at that moment. The first thing she saw was Dick riding atop his big old John Deere, proud and erect. He must have seen Hannah push back the curtains in her bedroom because in that instant, as she stood there with the slip dangling from her aging fingertips, Dickie Boy saluted and waved at his momma, and then he turned and rode off into the distance, the golden crops waving all around him.

Now if the story ended there, you'd say, Big deal. But there's more to it. Some folks don't believe this part. They say to me, "Gordon, you don't really believe that crazy legend, do you?" But they don't know the Nixons the way I knew them.

Here's what happened next. After Hannah's underwear found its way back onto her dresser, nothing more was said about the incident. But then one morning old Frank went out to the barn and found Dick out there with the tractor. Frank hollered out when he saw his son—because Frank Nixon wasn't the kind of man to contain his emotions too well—and when he yelled, Hannah came running. Frank tried but was not able to rush to the door fast enough to stop his wife and keep her from seeing their son in the grips of the devil's embrace.

There he was. Young Dick Nixon. A fifteen-year-old farm boy. Bright kid. Sweet kid. Frank and Hannah's kid. There he was in full costume—panties, bra, lipstick, black stockings, and a high-heeled shoe dangling from his big toe. He was hanging in a sitting position with a harness wrapped around his neck, and the harness was clipped to a rope that was hooked to the raised shovel attachment on the backhoe part of the tractor. One of his hands was reaching for the backhoe's control lever, and the other was thrust into his panties, grabbing at his you-know-what. The tractor's engine was still idling when the Nixons found their son.

Somehow, Dick was supposedly oblivious to the fact that his parents were there watching him, and so he just went ahead and yanked that backhoe lever one last time right in their presence. His poor momma fainted into her husband's arms on the spot.

Now let me tell you, that family was never the same again. Everyone around here noticed the change that came over the Nixons. Some people deny that it had anything to do with the tractor incident, and who knows, maybe there's more to the story than we found out through the grapevine. But either way, that boy caused some horrible hardships for his people back here in this quiet little Quaker community, and I say, he deserved whatever happened to him.

The Date

Her name was Vera Louise. She had the tiniest set of breasts Dick had ever seen. Some girls might have worn them like an apology. But not Vera Louise. The pointy little tips of her baby boobettes smiled at the world with every cheer she cheered on the sidelines at the football games.

Dick watched her from his permanent spot on the bench. He was an invaluable blocking dummy in practice and a reliable water boy during the games, but he never saw much playing time, so there was plenty of opportunity to memorize the contours of Vera Louise's angular bounceless titties.

The guys on the team knew Dick had a thing for Vera. They ribbed him about it constantly. And one day Henry Dade, the team captain and a defensive lineman, asked Dick if he'd like to be set up with Vera and her pouty little chest.

"My sister's best friends with her sister," Dade said. "I could fix it so you could take her out one night."

"You mean on a date?" Dick asked, leaning against his locker for support, like he'd just had the wind knocked out of him.

"No, you butthead, I thought maybe you'd like to teach her how to do a roll block."

"What I mean is, do you really think she'd want to go out with a guy like me? I'm not even a starter. I've only been in on three plays all year. She probably doesn't know who I am."

"I don't know about that," said Henry, "I seen her looking you over in practice one day. Her and her friends were pointing at you and giggling."

"And you think that might be a good sign?"

"Of course." And with that, Henry Dade walked off to his class, saying, "I'll look into it for you, Iron Butt."

It was nearly three whole days of endless agony before Henry Dade mentioned the date again. Dick hadn't said a word about it to anyone. He didn't want to foul it up. After all, it was awfully nice of Henry to do this for him, and he didn't want to be a nag about it. Dick had always suspected that Dade liked him more than the other guys on the team. When they all tackled Dick after practice, held him down and spit in his mouth, it was always Dade who made sure they only spat one time each.

It was a Thursday when Henry Dade sat down next to Iron Butt Nixon in the cafeteria and told him Vera Louise had said yes. Yes. She had said yes. "She wants you to pick her up at 7:30 on Friday. Wear a jacket and tie and take her someplace special 'cause she said she's got a new dress she wants to wear for you."

How could it be that Vera Louise, that sweet cheerleading goddess, wanted to go out on a date with Dick Iron Butt Nixon? How could it be? Was the world suddenly turning into the sane place it should have been all along? This was better than winning the election for class treasurer. It was better than winning a championship debate. It was better than beating Harold at tennis. This was what it was all supposed to be about. Me and Vera Louise, Dick thought. Me and her together on a date on Friday night.

It was only 7:05 when Dick pulled up in front of Vera's house with his suit coat pressed and his tie knotted tight around his thin little neck. Clutching a small bouquet of wild flowers he'd picked from behind the Grocery, he sat sweating in his father's pick-up truck, watching his watch, counting the beats of his heart.

He imagined his fingers gently brushing against Vera's pointy nipples. He imagined them hardening the way Harold had described it. His groin stirred. He readjusted himself, scared now that his hard-on might not go down in time for him to knock on Vera's screen door and call out her name at 7:30. He concentrated hard on limp thoughts. He conjured up his hate for Harold, his fear of his father, his love of argument. Still the boner sprang to attention, defying the weight of these things.

Limpness evaded him until he stopped trying to make it happen. He stopped fighting it. He let himself think of Vera Louise: first those breasts, but then her eyes—the clearest, most pure sapphire eyes God ever set in a woman's head. Vera's eyes were warm ice, an arctic fire, a haven in his adolescent hell. Thinking about her eyes was the thing that finally softened his rock hard penis. He checked his watch and picked at his underwear. A trickle of sweat ran down his butt crack.

God, he couldn't take the waiting anymore! He'd only wait a few more minutes. He'd give himself thirty seconds to make his way to the front porch. That way, he'd be sure to be on time, or perhaps even a few seconds early. He didn't mind if Vera knew he was eager. In fact, part of him wanted her to know. He was sure Vera Louise was the kind of girl who would appreciate honesty. But what if she was the kind of girl who liked the upper hand, he wondered. He decided that would be okay with him. He could play that role if that's what she wanted.

He wiped his brow with his handkerchief, then checked himself in the rearview mirror. If not for that damn buggy running over his head when he was a baby, he'd be able to part his hair on the side like all the other guys. Old scar head, old Iron Butt Scar Head. Oh well, Vera had already seen him. She had said yes. There was nothing to worry about.

The rusty door of the pick-up creaked open. Dick Nixon stepped out. Shoes shined. Hair slick. Shoulders back. Flowers in hand.

On the front porch, Dick knocked tentatively. He could hear soft nervous giggles coming from somewhere deep inside the house.

Maybe Vera was just as scared as he was. He knocked again, a little louder this time. "Coming," a woman's voice called. Dick swallowed hard and gave out a weak little whimper.

The woman standing at the door, wiping her hands on a dish rag, had to have been Vera Louise's lovely mother, a goddess in her own right—same narrow hips, same pointy boobs. Through the screen, he couldn't tell about the eyes. Her slender buttery voice said, "Oh my. What can I do for you, young man?"

Strange that she didn't realize who he was here to see, thought Dick. "I'm here to see Vera Louise," he said, summoning courage to his crackling vocal chords.

"Hmm. Well, let me go find her for you." The woman disappeared, calling from room to room, "Vera. Vera, you have a visitor." Dick was still standing on the porch, flowers in hand, waiting to be invited inside.

It was years before Vera showed her face at the door, but when she did, Dick began to wish it had been decades, even lifetimes. Something was terribly wrong. Vera Louise came bouncing into the hall and then stopped dead in her tracks. She was wearing cutoff shorts and a ragged cotton blouse. There were dirt rings around her ankles. She stepped toward the door, squinted out through the screen, then looked past Dick into the street behind him as if she were looking for someone or something that might help explain what was going on.

"Who are you?" she said.

It was at this moment that Dick Nixon discovered there could be no emotion more painful than embarrassment. Regret could make you feel as if you'd been transformed into a syrupy pile of steaming yellow vomit. It was flight-or-fight time.

"I'm Dick Nixon," he said. "We have a date."

"We do?" she said. "Says who?"

That's when the whole cruel world caved in on itself and there was nothing left but Dick's pathetic scar-headed self, standing in his own foolish puddle of sweat, holding flowers for a girl who didn't even know his name. He had reached the point of no return. Dick's adolescent self, with all its insecurities and fears and hate, curled up in a quivering fetal ball somewhere down inside the little toe on his left foot—not dormant, just hiding, full of resentment, waiting for revenge. In the years that would follow this moment, Dick Nixon would weigh every major crisis he encountered next to this one. None would compare.

He turned and began his retreat down the creaking wooden steps. Each step drew him closer to the self he thought he would escape when he held Vera Louise's hand in his own. Each step pushed him toward home, where Harold and his parents would be waiting. Each step took another bite out of him until at the bottom of the stoop, there was nothing left of him. It was worse than being alone. It was nonexistence. It was like being invisible, staring into the face of forever.

Then just as he began his unconscious stride toward the family truck, he heard the angel's voice call out. "Say, aren't you that kid they call Iron Butt?"

It wasn't much, but it was something. Dick hesitated, then turned and said, "Yes. That's me."

A silence settled between them, and Iron Butt waited—the cicadas buzzing in the trees all around them. Vera opened the screen door and stepped out onto the porch.

"What were you gonna do with those flowers?" Vera asked.

"They're for you," Dick said, holding them up.

"Gee, that's awful nice of you. Why don't you come around back and sit a spell." Vera Louise smiled. But Dick could see the charity in her blue eyes even from this distance.

"Thanks anyway," he said. And then he dropped the flowers at his feet, nodded at the thin shadowy figure there on the porch, and walked back to the truck. He drove away from Vera's house in a sad cloud of dust and vowed never to speak to her again.

The Debate

Resolved; That insects are more beneficial to man than harmful.

Dick stepped up to the podium. It squeaked. He set his note cards down on the podium. They were blank. He had nothing to say. Knew not a single damn thing about insects. His father was in the back of the room. He was here to observe his son, the youngest debater on the varsity team.

With all the craziness lately—taking care of the store, cooking for Pa and his brothers, studying for classes, going to visit Momma and Harold—Dick just didn't get the time to prepare for this debate. And now here he was standing at the podium, clearing his throat, and looking out at his fellow debaters and the judges and his father. They were all waiting. Even the chalk dust seemed to stand still in the air, waiting for Dick Nixon to say something important about insects. Something affirmative about the creatures that helped to destroy his father's lemon grove back in Yorba Linda.

One of the judges scribbled something. Dick cleared his throat again, lifted his blank note cards, and pretended to read them. He began: "Insects. The caterpillar, the daddy longlegs. The praying mantis." He was stalling. "The opposition would have us believe that the only function of an insect is to annoy man. The insect as nuisance, is the picture they paint. But let's take a moment to reflect on the insect's other functions, those which are practical and those which might be considered more symbolic."

He shuffled the first blank note card into the pile and took a deep breath. He had no idea what would come out of his mouth next. But he knew one thing for sure, the symbolic argument was the way to go. He could make up some good shit about that right here on the spot. The dangerous argument was the one about practical functions of the insect. That one could get him in trouble. He'd have to make up sources and everything. He calculated the risk, noticed his father scratching his chin, and plunged on.

"The black-tailed moss walker is an insect with which few of us here in the West are familiar. It is common to more humid and varied climates than our own." He was making it up. There was no such bug, of course. "The moss walker has two functions. First, it eats moss. Now, this may seem inconsequential to the untrained insect-hating human. But according to the *Encyclopedia Americana,* moss is known to be a fertile breeding ground for hypocalinod-rionic bacteria, which can cause lockjaw and even death to humans. So you see, by eating moss, the moss walker is providing a vital service to mankind."

In the back of the room, Dick's father sat motionless. He didn't budge. The judges scribbled. Other debaters were quietly searching through their notes. Dick suddenly remembered something from biology class. He continued: "Now let's consider an even more hated insect than the moss walker. All of us are familiar with the common maggot. This is a creature, like lice and the leech, which has received much ridicule in today's debate. But perhaps we would be less likely to attack these insects if we knew more about them. For instance, since Napoleonic times, maggots have been known to be capable of healing the most horrible of lacerations on both humans and animals. Your average everyday maggot feeds on dead flesh. They are not fond of live flesh for some unknown reason. And so a school of maggots exposed to an open wound will eat away at the dead flesh until only live, healthy flesh is exposed." One of the judges winced but kept scribbling. Dick was rolling now. He needed a kicker before he moved on to the symbolic part of the argument. "In addition," he said, shuffling his blank cards again, "when maggots defecate, that is to say, when they rid themselves of solid waste material, they release an antibody known to be an incomparable aid in healing. So you see, even the excrement of the lowly maggot can help man."

He had them now. All he had to do was finish it off. On to the symbolism. The easy part. Symbolism schmimbolism. Blah blah blah. He told them the insect represented the struggles of Man, the belief in the betterment of the society. He cited the colonial habits of the ant, the mating season of the cicada, the survival instinct of the mosquito. "These creatures," he argued, "remind us every day of what we are, what we were, what we might become, and for this, if for no other reason, they must be recognized as being beneficial to the human race despite the fact that we might find their appearance or behavior to be ugly." Blah blah blah. They ate it up. He even found the courage to slam his blank note cards down on the podium emphatically in midargument to pretend he was now so inspired that he would finish the remainder of his speech extemporaneously.

In the truck on the way home, Frank Nixon said nothing. He stared straight ahead, tight-lipped, hands clenched. Dick sat next to him with the first-place trophy in his lap. Finally, when Dick could take the silence no longer, he said, "So what did you think of my speech, Pa?"

Frank looked at Dick and then back at the road ahead. For a long minute, Frank said nothing, and Dick began to think he would say nothing all the way home, but finally, Frank said this: "My son, you talk out of your butt. If you are a true Nixon, you'll stick that trophy in the garbage as soon as we get home."

Dick could physically feel the heat inside him. There was a magnetic field in his chest and it was reversing its pull. Every piece of hate he'd stored up inside that field was loosening up, freeing itself from the gravity that had kept it contained these past sixteen years. It consumed him, rearranged his identity, made him all one thing and a thousand things at once. He was broken bits of the past on fire. There was no way to stop the rage.

For once in his life, Dick wanted to say, "Listen, you old fuck, they call me Iron Butt Nixon. You know why? I'll tell you why. Because I study so fucking hard. Because I'm good at what I do, and I got that way by earning it. Because I play to win. Because I am a winner. I'm a success, old man. And it's about time you pat me on the fucking back, and say, 'Nice job, Dick m'boy. Nice job.' "

He didn't say these things though. He just glared at his father, hoping to bore a hole through him with his angry eyes.

Dick really did want to let the old bastard have it—tell Frank in classic Iron Butt fashion, point by point, what an asshole he was. He glanced down at the trophy in his lap, then back at Frank. For a split second he thought he could see a cruel little smirk on his father's face. And in that instant, Dick was sure his father could read his mind.

Frank was just testing him, Dick thought, like always. Everything was a test, a preparation of some sort. Frank was seeing how far Dick could be pushed. Dick knew then that he wouldn't give the old man the satisfaction of launching him over the edge. He'd keep it cool, reel himself back together, rise above the anger.

Dick would prove once and for all to his father and himself that he was ready for the world outside Whittier, which would, no doubt, be full of assholes like Frank Nixon.

At home later that afternoon, Dick did in fact throw the trophy in the garbage. But a day later, it showed up on the top shelf behind the counter in the grocery store. Polished and shined for all the customers to see—Dick's disgrace on display for all of Whittier. Frank never said another word about the trophy, but whenever a customer commented on it, he smiled his mean little smile as if to say, That's Richard's. He won it for talking out of his ass.

Grocery

In the grocery business, you usually have two enemies. The food and the customers. If your boss is an asshole, you've got three enemies. If the asshole boss is your father, you can count him as a double enemy because you have to go home with him at the end of the day. If your asshole boss father is as big an asshole to the customers as he is to you, you've got to make friends with your second enemy, the customers, so you can help keep the family business afloat. If driving into town in the family truck to pick up a week's supply of head lettuce is your only opportunity to get out of the store, then your first enemy, the food, becomes your best friend.

Dick treated the heads of lettuce with great respect. He'd rinse them with a garden hose before he brought them into the store. He'd prune back their wilted leaves. He'd pick the dirt crumbs off them like a mother monkey cleaning her young. The lettuce was his friend. And if a head sat too long on the shelf, turned pink and then brown, and no one showed any interest in it, Dick grieved for it. But he rejoiced too, for a shortage of lettuce at week's end meant another trip into town, another morning away from the store.

In the truck, he hummed along with the radio, smiling wide, as clouds of dust billowed around him and the tires labored through gravel tracks. It's not that Dick was afraid of work. On the contrary, old Iron Butt loved it. Work was the one thing he was always sure of. Something you could always count on—a time when your sweat was admired. He could get lost in work; the repetition of a task sent him away to a place within himself and outside himself at the same time. It was a place where thought and emotion were so intertwined that they were indistinguishable as separate entities. It was a place of secrecy where every thought and its opposing counterthought made perfect sense. Here you could debate yourself for hours and never lose, no matter which side you defended.

So it wasn't work which Dick needed to escape from on those hot California mornings when he went to town for iceberg lettuce. The road that led to Whittier also led past it, into the whole un-known world beyond the state line, beyond mom-and-pop gro-ceries and withering citrus farms and bubbling oil wells that should have been yours—the world that called to Dick every time he set a can on a shelf or scrubbed a mare or cracked open another schoolbook. Like the train whistle he heard at night outside his bedroom window—the Santa Fe line. Everything around him seemed to be calling him east, where dignified men wore black suits every day and got paid for their thoughts.

The road to the produce supplier was well traveled, worn and ditched. But Dick didn't expect a smooth ride. He hummed all the way into town. There was more to it than just lettuce, of course. There were peaches, oranges, and all the rest. The truck swelled, its bed overflowing with delights so pure it was hard to believe they were of the earth. The food was not Dick's enemy. It was his savior.

All morning back at the store, Frank Nixon tried to ignore his bleeding ulcers and growled at customers, slapping boxes onto the shelves Dick usually stocked. Dick would be back from town in time to finish up the dry goods load and still get to school early. After school, it would be football or violin lessons or debate prac-tice, and then finally he'd be back at the store to finish the day's stock work. At the end of the long day, Dick would rather lie in the cool grass and dream of the future. But there would be more work that needed doing, and by that time of day, Frank Nixon would have turned off his hearing aid and he'd be yelling at customers just for fun.

"The world's no place for a dreamer!" Frank would yell. "Get that little Quaker butt of yours in here 'fore I tan you bloody, boy."

Hannah Nixon wanted her Richard to be a missionary in Central America. But there would be plenty of time for that later. For now she knew he was the buffer that could save the family grocery. Whenever Frank went into one of his tirades, like calling Gladys Swanson the devil's cheerleader for requesting fresher milk, or like stomping up the vegetable aisle to confront Brother Timmons about something his son said in Sunday school, Richard intervened, a missionary on a mission. This was tricky business because Frank was a man who handled his own affairs. The best thing to do was to prevent the confrontations before they happened. Richard got quite good at spotting a potential problem as soon as it walked into the store.

Richard's older brother Harold spent his afternoons playing tennis on a nearby dirt court or sitting in the clubhouse out back, writing poems to girls from school. Frank never worked Harold very hard, what with the TB and all. Besides, Dick could handle it.

The first summer that Hannah took Harold off to the lungers' colony in Prescott, Arizona, was when everything changed at the Nixon Grocery. Business picked up. The customers grew to like Frank Nixon much better, and Dick rarely had to mediate between his father and a customer anymore. Some said Hannah's going away was the best thing that ever happened to Frank. But they weren't in Dick's shoes.

In the morning, it was Dick who dragged his father out of bed rather than the other way around. Frank was only half a man without Hannah, silenced by loneliness. When he turned off his hearing aid, it wasn't because he wanted to yell without interruption; it was more because he wanted to be left alone, lost in his self-pity.

One day trying to get a rise out of his father, Dick said, "I hear Thompson wants to raise the price on his tomatoes again." But Frank did not respond. He was trapped in his own silent head, mooning for Hannah, worrying about Harold.

That night, over their usual dinner of canned beans and fried eggs, a dinner Dick cooked for them, Frank told Dick they were going to close the store for the weekend and make the fifteen-hour drive through the desert to Prescott to see Harold and Hannah. Saying it aloud made it so and Frank smiled. It was the first smile Dick had seen on his father's face in over a month.

But the trip was all car ride and not much visit, and with all the lungers about, there was no telling what any of them might catch. There was nowhere for the children to play. Dick spent the days in the cabin studying for an upcoming debate. At night, Harold told Dick about some girl at the lungers' colony with extraordinarily large breasts. "They feel like jelly in a bag," Harold said.

When it seemed everyone was finally asleep, Dick lay awake, staring at the ceiling, thinking about jelly breasts, wondering if he could get away with touching himself with Harold beside him. He lay silent, listening to the crickets and cicadas in the distance. Mingled with the insect cries was another familiar sound. From somewhere inside that cabin, he was sure he heard the anxious whispers of his parents. He even thought he heard his own name on their lips.

When they got back to Whittier early Monday morning, having driven through the night to get there in time to open the store, Frank turned off his hearing aid again, and went about the business of sweeping the store. In slow, silent arcs his broom stirred the dust into lazy storms that fluttered and then settled here and there about the floor in halfhearted, unorganized piles. In this way he moved around the store all day, staring down at the bristles of his broom as they swept and stirred, swept and stirred. Dick watched him doing this until the sun set late on that July evening, and not once did Frank Nixon bend down to gather up a pile of the dust he had spent all day sweeping.

The next morning, Frank told Dick to pack his things. He was sending him off to Prescott to help Hannah and Harold make ends meet. The Nixon Grocery would have to survive without him.

The Laundromat

Ray Carver and his daughter Julia usually watched the evening news while they ate their TV dinners—Salisbury steak, creamed corn, and hot pudding in foil trays. Something about the Apollo program was always on. Lunar landing, Kennedy saying Nixon would never have followed through with NASA the way he had, and all of that. Ray's little girl made blast off noises while she watched the galactic news clips and picked at her corn. But none of that is what this is about. Not directly anyway. This is about what happened to Ray one Saturday afternoon in a laundromat.

It was the only laundromat in town. The Spin Cycle it was called. Ray was by himself. Little Julia was at a bowling alley with some friends. Ray had no idea where Peggy was or who she was with. The point is, it was Ray's turn to do the laundry—soiled Disney underwear, t-shirts spotted with multiple Kool Aid stains in varying shades and hues, bibs, overalls, party dresses, etc.

So he was sitting there, watching the clothes go round, waiting for a dryer, keeping an eye on the clock because Julia would need to be picked up soon. He was trying to read a book—some trashy suspense thing somebody had left on the folding table. He had a huge pile of wet stuff in his laundry cart. He was literally the only man in the place except for a deranged-looking guy in the corner who was licking a patty-melt-to-go from Norm's Grill across the street.

A dryer opened up. Ray got up to roll his cart over there, but some Madonna cut in front of him and took his machine. He'd been waiting longer than she. "I only have one small load," she said. "It'll be quick. Gee, you've got quite a bit there, haven't you?" she said. This wasn't the first dryer Ray had missed out on. He wanted to strangle her with a soggy sock, but she had nice calves, so he let it slide.

Ray went back to his book. Two women beside him were talking about a third woman's hysterectomy. A large brown rat scurried behind two washing machines. For the moment the rat meant nothing to Ray. His mind was on other things: the detective in the novel he was reading who called every woman Sweetstuff, Julia who would be waiting for him shortly, his wet clothes dripping through the cart onto the floor, and the pennant-race chances of the Chicago Cubs.

Once a rat came into Ray's apartment over on Keeler Ave. Peggy beat it to death with a broom while Julia and he ate Spaghetti-O's and looked on. The TV was playing in the background. Another launch attempt was being made. Or maybe it was a rerun of a previous launch. At any rate, the announcer was counting down, 10-9-8-7 . . . and so forth, as Peggy beat the life out of the rat. They were in sync, the announcer and Ray's wife. Him counting, her slugging, like lovers in rhythm, Peggy and her NASA stud.

Ray went back to his book. On the other side of the laundromat, the door swung open and a little kid about Julia's age came in with a mangy mutt on a leash. She walked over to the gumball machine and dropped in a penny. She rifled gumballs into her mouth like there was no tomorrow, until she ran out of pennies. The patty-melt slurper in the corner mumble-shouted at her. "Hey, kid, get out of here with that dog. This ain't no place for animals."

The kid shuffled out. On the other side of the storefront window, she stuck her rainbow-colored gumball tongue out at him and pressed it hard against the dirty glass. Then she and the dog ran off, giggling and barking respectively. The man grumbled something Ray couldn't understand and went back to his burger.

Out of the blue, one of the hysterectomy ladies leaned in close to Ray and had the nerve to say, "I hope you don't think you're going to use more than one dryer. I mean, I realize you have quite a large load there, but there are several of us waiting, you know." Ray didn't say anything. He just stared at the pages of his book.

Finally, next to him, a dryer slowed to a dying tumble. He checked the wall clock. Julia would need to be picked up very soon. If no one came to get those clothes out in three minutes, he was going to dump them onto the folding table himself and worry about apologies later.

A minute or two went by. He was practically salivating. He wanted that dryer bad. He'd stuff all three of his loads into it if he had to, and he'd put about ten dimes in the damn thing and just let it go, read his book, keep an eye on the clock. There might still be enough time.

Two more dryers opened up on the other side of the room, but the hysterectomy twins snagged them. Ray slammed his book down on the bench. That's when the derranged burger slurper came over and sat down beside him.

"Don't feel bad," the slurper said. "I know just how it is." He crossed his legs tightly like a woman wearing a short skirt. Then, swatting the air in front of his face, he said, "Mind if I join you?"

Ray grunted a response that could have been read as yes or no, depending on the perceptiveness of the recipient.

The guy went on. "When I was a boy," he said, "I always knew when the grass needed to be cut."

"Oh," Ray said.

"The Good Humor Man. That's how I knew. Those dream-sicle bars. The ones with the orange popsicle on the outside and the vanilla ice cream inside. I'd hear the bells. Dusk. That's when you mow. Grass stands at attention at the end of a clear day. All that sun. And it's cooler then, so the ice cream don't melt so fast. We could smell the neighborlady's cigarette smoke coming from the porch stoop next door. And the fireflies. We'd smash them in mid-air with baseball bats." He nudged Ray with his elbow, then tugged on his ear lobes. He smelled of urine.

"Kids," he said, pointing to Julia's underthings in his basket. Ray didn't say anything.

"Yep," he said, "I know."

Ray picked up his book and thumbed through, pretending to be looking for his place.

The big brown rat reappeared then, poking its snout out from behind a washer. It looked both ways, made sure the coast was clear, and scurried toward Ray and his new companion. Ray was startled to see this rat coming right at him with such determination. But then it changed direction ever-so-slightly, as if to relieve Ray of his fear. The next thing Ray knew, the rat was circling around the ankles of the burger-eating philosopher of the lawn.

The rat nuzzled against the man's feet, purring like a hungry kitten. The rat did perfect figure eights around and between the man's legs. They were old friends, the man and this rat.

"Hungry little devils," the man said, reaching inside his jacket. He brought out a French fry, tore it into pieces, and fed the rat by hand, one nibble at a time until the rat's flabby back twitched and its tail jerked from side to side. The man brushed the fry grease off on his trousers.

"Well, I can see you got work to do. I'll let you be." He stood then and saluted. The rat scurried back behind the washing machine. "Don't forget," the man said. "Dusk."

"Right. Dusk," Ray said. "I won't forget."

He winked at Ray and ambled out the door.

Ray sat for a minute with his book on his lap. The women around the room were tending their business—stopping to pick up a dropped sock, reaching into a pile for its matching foot, reading the side of a bleach bottle, counting coins, bitching about impotent husbands, folding jeans, drinking Pepsi, eating a Hershey bar. And in the universe behind the washers and dryers, families of rats were going about their routine too, doing whatever it is rats do when they cross "begging for fries" off their To-Do list.

A too-thin woman in her late thirties suddenly walked up and opened the stopped dryer Ray had been waiting for. She reached in, pulled something out, testing it for dampness. A few oily strands of her dark hair fell into her eyes. She brushed them back with her hand, but they fell again. She reached into the dryer once more and felt around. The clothes must have been a little damp still because she emptied the lint trap, dropped another coin in the slot, and closed the dryer door.

Ray checked the other dryers around the room. Still full. And their users stood ready with pockets full of shiny Roosevelt dimes. He'd never finish the laundry in time. Julia would be waiting. The clothes dripped in the basket.

The clothes would stay damp. Ray would be late. Dinner would be late too, and it would be out of a can or a frozen package again. The carpet would need vacuuming. And the grass—mowing. Later that night, Julia would undoubtedly interrupt another feeble attempt at romance. Tomorrow, they'd be out of Band-Aids and the Radio Flyer would lose a wheel and the mail would bring another electric company threat. This was Ray's whole life dripping away in the basket, forever waiting for a dryer.

Ray thought of all the other lives he might have lived if not for his daughter and Peggy, if not for a lot of things. He could have done something different, something that would have mattered, could have been a teacher, a lawyer, a poet, anything. If circumstances had been different, who knows how his life might have turned out? Somehow, that day Ray came to see that his life had been just a series of forced compromises.

He wondered if he had it in him to show his daughter there was another way. Maybe that would be what he had to offer. Maybe one day when Julia had an impossible marriage of her own, she'd call him up looking for advice, and he'd tell her something fit for a bumper sticker. A bootstrap slogan. "Get your priorities straight, Sweetheart. Aim your sights higher. Shoot for the moon, Baby Doll." But of course, he'd know, and so would Julia by then, that there's nothing up there on that dusty old gray rock but a limp American flag, hiding its impotence with a coat hanger. A very small step for mankind.

In Those Days

In those days, when you were part of a large family, a large farm family especially, what with illness, chores, climatic extremes, and other hardships, you didn't think about your own desires, your own dreams. You just did what you were told. It was like being a flywheel in a big tractor, spinning around and around again, trying not to spoil the momentum for the throttle and the governor and the other moving parts which were trying just as hard as you to make the tractor go. And every few minutes, some son of a bitch would come along and throw gravel into the most delicate of the moving parts, but you couldn't even stop to dust it out. You just cranked the gravel through and whatever damage the tractor incurred you'd have to deal with later. If there was ever time. If you ever finished the damn harvest.

Those were the days when a baby would nearly split his poor mother in half coming through the canal. No Demerol back then. Momma hollered her head off when Dick squirmed his way into the world—an ungrateful eleven-pound, fat-headed freak with bloody black curls clinging to his scalp as he poked out for a peek at civilization.

She nearly died before the head even came through, her skin stretching and ripping down there, and him in a big fucking hurry to present himself to the waiting world. Then, finally a momentary relief from the pain. A sloshing pop as he wiggled his chin through and she tightened around his neck. Not tight enough though and he kicked and she pushed involuntarily, and then those fleshy shoulders of his. Oh, it was just too much. Momma finally passed out from the agony.

When she awoke, there hanging from the forceps, there he was, her little man, jowled already and screaming like no Milhous nor no Nixon before him had ever screamed. Born in the house his father built from a Sears Roebuck kit. Born during a rare cold snap with all that fog in the fields and all that blubber on his bones. And that cavernous whole in the middle of his crazy oblong face opened again and again as he screamed his little lungs out into the damp Yorba Linda night.

So when his momma moved off to a higher, drier elevation to take care of his sickly older brother, and she asked him to come out for the summer to help her make ends meet, he figured it was the least he could do. He owed her that much and a whole lot more. And if she could stand taking care of three bedridden patients—cooking and cleaning, wiping out bedpans, giving bed baths and alcohol rubs—and if she could stand watching them die off one by one, knowing her eldest son might be next, then Dick could stand to pluck chickens or work at the carnival or mop out urinals or whatever else it took to help her pay the bills. She needed him. And that's all there was to it. That's the way it worked in those days.

Stoop labor they called it. Fifty cents a day, if you were lucky. Stooping in the muck of somebody else's orders. Field gnats flying up your nose. The fluttering little bastards squirming down into your throat.

The boss man barks at you, "Get this do that shut the fuck up and work you little pansy. Mush doggie mush!" He barks until you can't take it anymore. You're on your knees, and you want to bark back, but you know you can't because Momma's in the cabin nursing your brother and they're counting on you, or rather on the fifty cents you're going to bring home at the end of the day.

It's 110 degrees and there you are digging a ditch or stacking bricks or shoveling manure and there's the boss man, high atop his mighty mare, and he hawks up a loogie and it lands, thwap, right in the middle of your sweaty back and you can feel it sliding down your spine, dribbling toward your butt crack, and you suddenly remember you're a Nixon—not the firstborn of course, but a Nixon nonetheless, and no one spits on a Nixon. So that's it. You break.

You rise from your knees slowly, deliberately. The boss man barks again but you can't even hear what he's saying now. You're too lost in your own fury. It bubbles up on you frothy and bloody. You blurt out something even you don't quite fully understand. You say, "Bend over, boss man, cause in my next life, I'm going to do the barking, you swine-faced asshole fuck. And you'll be on *your* knees sucking on *my* manure. Right up your ever-loving ass, you jag bag."

A pregnant moment passes. The boss man's mouth is open, his eyebrows ajar. You push your shoulders back as you feel the boss man's loogie slithering into your shorts. Then you stomp off his field with pride. No longer stooped. Standing tall. And for that one small moment, you aren't a slave anymore to the way things are these days.

Wheel of Fortune

Waves of color float on barkers' voices and calliope melodies. Sinners live in color. They gamble a day's wages and ogle at sideshow freaks. Siamese brothers. Fat women in lusty feather robes. A two-headed calf. Hey mister, knock the milk bottle down and win a Kewpie doll.

"Step right up, folks. Step right up to Dick's Wheel of Fortune. Try your luck." Luck, which these bastards have too much of, thinks Dick. Luck, which has escaped the clutches of every Milhous and every Nixon at every turn. Even the luckiest son of a bitch of the whole pack, the favorite son, Harold Milhous Nixon himself, was at this very moment back in his cot at the cabin with a cool rag on his head, his fever rising. Some luck.

Still, sympathy aside, Dick hated Harold. Hated him beyond hate. Beyond the heated hate of childhood to an icy numb that hurt more than hot hate. But of course Quakers aren't allowed to hate. Quakers can rise above it. They live in monochrome.

Good Quaker mothers pray alone in the closet at night. They lock themselves in there and pray in the old tongues. Pray that their sons live forever and know no hate.

A good Quaker son goes to Arizona every summer to help his momma by bringing home fifty cents at the end of every day. He earns it any way he can. Any way the townies will let him. Any way that doesn't kill him. Even if it means barking at gamblers, selling demon greed to sinners who want something for nothing.

"Step right up," he'd bark. And they'd bark back, "Shut up and spin the wheel, you dumb fathead!"

Balloons. That was the first thing Dick noticed the first time he went to Frontier Days to see about the barker job. Bloodred balloons filled with clean air. Sinners' air. From fresh, pink, godless lungs. Human helium. Dick was sure it was a trick they did. A pact with the devil. Give him your soul and your air will be lighter than air. Your lungs immune.

The balloons rose skyward, filled with sweet, foul sinner breath, tugging at the ends of their strings—a dance, a mating ritual—stretching toward God's wrinkled, unassuming feet.

A little girl in a yellow dress walked by, innocent enough, sucking on a giant pink cotton ball. A balloon tied to her wrist. If she's not careful, Dick thought, that balloon will carry her off into the heavens where God might mistake her for just another sinner. A pigtailed little sinner floating above the clouds. The devil's child trying to sneak through God's iron gates.

She sauntered and swaggled like the hussy she would someday become, and in that instant, she brushed past Dick. She had no way of knowing he was a Milhous Nixon; no way of knowing he was here about the barker job, here in Prescott to spin the wheel of fortune and help Mother Milhous make ends meet while Brother Harold lay dying at the Pinecrest lungers' colony. To this small girl in the yellow dress, Dick was invisible. He imagined he was cotton candy melting in her small mouth, dissolving on her pink tongue, turning into sugary goo on her taste buds.

Dick's groin had a mind of its own. It stirred, tugged. It had a sinner's mind. For God's sake, she's just a little girl, he told himself. He reminded himself that he was nearly seventeen, nearly grown, capable of splitting this child in half. But she was watermelon ash, candy apple feces, saffron rock. A sweet and sour taste that he imagined would arouse an unsightly puckering grimace. A sinner's smile. Soon she would become another nasty little Glenda

Newcomb, lifting her floral print dress high up over her head so the likes of Brother Harold could see the whole sunwashed universe there in her devilish crotch.

The Wheel of Fortune was Dick's domain. The most popular attraction at the fair. "Step right up, folks. Try your luck on the wheel." They stepped up in droves. Old men and little girls alike. Ready to throw away a penny or even a whole nickel on a single go. Their coins felt good in Dick's pouch. Weighty and noisy and cold to the touch. The only relief in the Arizona heat. He pressed the cool quarters against his sweaty brow, sent little girls to the refreshment stand to get him a lemonade, told them he'd count to one hundred while they ran off with his money. None of them was ever stupid enough to return. But every day, he'd test another child. He wasn't searching for goodness. He was teaching himself a lesson.

Finally one day, he offered a lovely little girl a nickel to go get the lemonade and another nickel to return with it. No counting to one hundred. Just plain profit. The girl looked at him and said, "You're crazy, mister. But okay." And she did it. Took his nickel plus two pennies for the lemonade, came running back without spilling a drop, put out her hand for the other nickel, then tried to give him the piss yellow drink. But he refused. "No thanks," he said. "Never could stand lemonade."

So it went. Dick sweated and barked all summer. Sweated and barked alongside the freaks and geeks in the horror-show desert heat. Balloons floated away, loosened from the wrists of careless children. The calliope pumped its festival formula. And all the while Dick Nixon watched and learned. Learned how the world worked outside of Whittier, California. Learned what it meant to live in a Quakerless Neverland where people breathed helium and silver coins clinked in your pocket—more coins than you could ever imagine. Most importantly, he learned that if you barked loud enough and had something to offer, people listened, people responded. People came running.

Center Field

So there we were in the bleachers on the first-base side at Humbolt Park, waiting for the full-count delivery. The sun was burning my arms and some little kid was drooling a Popsicle down my back. It was the top of the first inning. This guy named McMillian was pacing the mound for the Cougars. He shook off a pitch, peeked over his shoulder, kicked, and all of the sudden, out of nowhere, as I raised my beer cup to my lips, Dick said, "Did you ever wonder if your wife is a lesbian?"

Ray and I just laughed and all three of us missed the pitch, which turned out to be ball four. "Sometimes I think Pat's a lesbian," Dick said. Then he said, "I don't know, maybe she's just some kind of amoeba creature."

"What's'a matter," Ray asked, "you ain't getting any?"

Dick didn't answer, just ignored Ray, which was all the same to me. I had come to watch a baseball game, frankly. But it didn't look like the Cougars were going to be *getting any* that afternoon either. They stunk, as usual. Still, there I was just like every year—sucking down beers and hoping for a miracle. Sitting between Dick and Ray gave me a sort of new perspective on the game, especially with Dick wearing his disguise.

Ray had convinced Dick that the only way he'd go unnoticed at the ball park was if he dressed like a complete nutcase. Protesting the whole time, Dick let himself be dressed in a T-shirt that said

"Bleacher Preacher" across the front and "Crusade for Baseball" on the back. On his head, Dick wore a safari hat with a propeller on top of it. The propeller was spinning like mad when Dick huffed, "I look like a moron."

"Better than looking like Dick Nixon," Ray said, and just for good measure, we put mirrored sunglasses and a fake beard on him too.

There was a good crowd on hand at Humbolt Park that day, it being Easter week and all. Way out in center field, there was some kind of crazy Mexican festival going on. They had all kinds of picnic tables and balloons and so forth. Dick pointed it out to us in the second inning and said, "Those people are always celebrating something." Then he added, "I hear their women fuck like rabbits."

"I guess they've got plenty to celebrate then," Ray said.

McMillian, the pitcher, laid a turd of a fastball over the heart of the plate, and some guy from the Roscoe Stars clobbered it into left for extra bases. We were off to a great start, as usual. "Boy oh boy, these guys sure are a bunch of losers," Dick said.

"It's just semipro," Ray said, "don't get all riled up."

"Baseball is baseball, Ray," Dick said, and just by the tone in his voice, we knew he was about to launch into a sermon worthy of the Bleacher Preacher label on his chest. "Baseball is about heartbreak, survival, history, getting on with it in spite of history, overcoming the odds in the bottom of the ninth with the bases loaded and two outs. That's what this fucking game is about. It's revolution. It's constitution." He was definitely living up to the name on his shirt. He went on: "Baseball is about passing on the best of what you are, the best of what *we* are, so that we might mutate into a better self, a better species. It's America reinventing itself. It's having nine lives to live every time you step out onto the field and you're reborn to the sound of the umpire shouting, 'Play ball.' It's a little kid watching the Red Sox one strike away from winning the World Series, and even though the ball rolls through Bill Buckner's legs, that little kid comes back to the ball park again the next year with his dad and roots for his Bosox all over again, and someday he'll tell his own son about the time he was at the World Series and it won't even matter anymore that the Sox blew it!" Dick was really rolling. I could see myself in his sunglasses.

"This game forgives," Dick said, his propeller momentarily stopped in the still summer air. "You think anybody cares that Mickey Mantle was a drunk or that Babe Ruth slept with floozies or that Phil Neikro put Vaseline on the bill of his cap? Baseball tolerates everything, but do these young players with their hotshot agents appreciate that? Of course not."

I tried to head him off at the pass. "When I was a little kid," I said, "my mother bought me a 3-D picture of Jesus to hang over my bed. She was a very religious woman, my mother. This 3-D picture looked like one of those baseball cards they used to give out free in boxes of Frosted Flakes. In the picture, Jesus was standing behind a little kid in a Cubs uniform. The kid was standing at home plate with a bat in his hand, but the bat looked way too big for him. So Jesus was standing behind him, helping him get a grip on the bat handle."

"Are you mocking me, kid?" Dick said.

"No, I swear. I know it sounds crazy. When I think about that picture now I sometimes wonder if maybe it was just something I saw in a feverish, childhood hallucination brought on by chicken pox or something. But it's not. I'm sure of it. I remember it as clear as can be."

When McMillian finally got the Cougars out of the second inning, I popped open another couple of beers, one for me and one for Dick. Minimal damage done—only three runs for the Stars. There was still plenty of time to make it up. But the Cougars left two men stranded in their half of the inning and didn't score. Already this game had all the makings of a lost cause, but I knew damn well we'd stay through to the end, sucking down beers and cheering every time this sorry bunch of losers gave us false hopes.

During the between-inning warm-ups, Dick said, "You hear about this Albert Belle character with the cork in his bat?"

Both Ray and I had heard the story. The sports columnists

were calling it "Batgate." We knew it was just a matter of time till Dick brought it up. Supposedly Belle, the Cleveland Indians slugger, had been caught using a corked bat in a game against the White Sox, and when the umpires confiscated the bat and locked it up, somebody broke in and stole it. It was a big scandal. Every baseball fan in the country had been talking about it for weeks.

"You know what I'd do if I were the baseball commissioner?" Dick said.

"Weren't you offered that job once?" Ray asked.

"Yeah, I was as a matter of fact, and if I were sitting in that job right now, here's what I'd do. First, I'd make Belle call his mother and explain, in detail, why he has grown up to be a cheat. Next, I'd make him write an open letter to all of America for treating the nation's pastime like an old whore. Then, I'd make Mr. Belle strip naked and I'd strap him to a billboard in downtown Cleveland in the middle of the winter, and I'd make him hold up a magnifying glass to his very small penis. And above his head, the billboard would read, 'Here's the real reason I filled my bat with cork!' "

Ray and I couldn't help but laugh.

Dick pounded his fist into his palm and went on. "In addition to the above punishments, I would, of course, ban Belle from baseball stadiums as a player or spectator for the rest of his natural life. And if anyone ever proves the theory of reincarnation, I would extend the ban to all creatures that share Albert Belle's new form. I realize this may seem harsh, but let me just say this, better to ban a few innocent dragonflies or sweat bees from major league stadiums than to take a chance on letting the likes of a reincarnated Albert Belle back into the graces of baseball!" With that, Dick thumped his fist down on the bench. Back on the field, a Cougar cracked a line drive into left field.

Ray said, "You would have made a fine baseball commissioner, Dick."

"You're goddamn right I would have. And you know what else? There wouldn't have been any players' strike on my watch either. These pansy-ass pud whackers are trying to hold the game hostage. But I'll tell you something, this is the only sport where the defense has control of the ball, and that's why there's still hope. The candy-ass motherfuckers who call themselves players just don't get it. Bunch of lily-livered putzes from their vanilla-frosted, aluminum-sided suburban houses with three fucking TVs on the wall like Elvis fucking Presley, flipping back and forth from Bart Simpson to Dan Rather to the Playboy Channel, until they get drafted into the minors where they chase hick broads in short skirts and drink Southern Comfort. And in a couple of years they end up making four million dollars to hit .265."

Before long three or four innings had slipped by and the Cougars had managed to leave something like eight or nine men stranded. But Dick was still on a roll, and the game didn't much matter anymore.

"You know, guys like Jimmy Piersall don't exist anymore," Dick said, popping open another beer. "That crazy fuck would have done anything for this game. He knew it was a religion. And Piersall knew *how* to worship. Climbed the backstop and howled like a wounded wolf when he struck out. Today's million-dollar pitcher couldn't pitch his way around Bob Uecker. But do they feel shame? No. They ask for a fucking raise, free agency, a guarantee of no salary cap."

Dick kept on ranting inning after inning, but at some point I did finally manage to tune him out. It's a pleasurable experience to sit in the bleachers with friends on a warm afternoon, but there comes a point when Dick is on one of these rampages, that you start to feel like a spectator at a masturbation exhibition. The best thing to do when this happens is draw his attention to something else.

The Cougars were still getting their asses kicked, so there was nothing on the playing field to distract him, but luckily, Ray had the wherewithal to thumb Dick's attention back out to center field where the Mexican Easter festival was going on. He said to Dick and me, "Hey, check it out."

By now, there was a big crucifix stuck in a mound of dirt out there, and the Mexicans were getting ready to strap some long-haired freak up on the thing. He was supposed to be Jesus. They were actually reenacting the crucifixion out there in center field, just beyond the home run fence. All the other Mexicans were just mingling around like it was a cocktail party or something. "They're out there looking to get lucky with some cousin's cousin, while Jesus bleeds to death," Dick said.

"Man, those deep-fried doughnut things they're eating look good, don't they?" Ray said.

"It's like nobody notices the poor son of a bitch up there in his little toga and crown of thorns," Dick said.

"Yeah, he's like a corpse at an Irish wake," Ray said.

"A sideshow attraction with fake Halloween blood dripping down his forehead," I said.

"You know, I wonder if anybody would think twice these days about crucifying some crazy bastard who says he's the son of God?" Ray said. "Who'd think twice?"

I looked around the bleachers, and as far as I could tell, we were the only dumb bastards watching Jesus up there on his big old crucifix. The guy had probably worked on his costume for weeks, but nobody even seemed to care.

"If there is a God," Dick said, "he's one warped son of a bitch."

"Yeah, but probably not warped enough to waste his time on the likes of us," Ray said.

"Speak for yourself, Ray," I said.

They both looked at me a little strange then, like they weren't sure if they'd heard me correctly or not. The game was winding down, and to be honest, I don't even remember what the score was at that point, but the fat lady was gargling with warm salt water, and it was only a matter of time.

Dick said, "You know, I don't *really* think Pat is a lesbian." And then he wondered aloud, "But what would a guy do if he got stuck with a lesbian for a wife?"

And Ray said, "I guess we all get what we deserve in this life."

Dick thought about this a minute and then spun the propeller on top of his safari hat and said, "At least I'm not wasting my days looking for the great paradise beyond. The kingdom of heaven or some such shit. I mean, look where it gets you—" he pointed to center field—"stuck on a cross, hoping some little senorita notices you, helps you down, dresses your wounds, feeds you grapes, and then sucks you off real good. A totally toothless blow job, all tongue and lips and suction, and a one-gulp swallow when it's over. Now that's what I call heaven. Paradise here on earth."

Smoking Gun

Here's how it happened. Harold had the hots for Jessie Lynch. This Lynch girl was a fellow lunger. Like Harold, Jessie Lynch knew what it meant to hack up wads of death every morning.

Back home, Harold got whatever or whoever he wanted. Any little hussy in Whittier would hold a rag on his forehead, kneel next to him in church, suck his cock, whatever. He was the pride of the town. Every Quaker girl's favorite impending tragedy. But Jessie was different. She had her own impending tragedy to live with and wasn't much impressed by Harold's. She was the first girl that didn't fall at his ugly bony feet and offer her services to him. Served him right. Everything usually came so fucking easy to Harold. Seems odd to say that about a man with the sins of humanity growing in his lungs, but that's the truth of the way it was.

Anyway, Harold wrote Jessie Lynch love notes from his smelly lunger's cot, while Momma Nixon draped him with blankets and damp rags. Jessie Jessie Jessie. He scribbled her name across the page for hours, coughing up into a kerchief as he curled the *J* into the *e* in her name. He moped and mooned over her all summer. Just wasn't himself.

What made matters worse was Larry Easton. Old Jessie had a wicked crush on Larry, another lunger who lived with Harold and Momma and Dick in the Prescott cabin. Momma took Larry in to help pay the bills at the hospital in Prescott. In those days, she was always taking other lungers in and playing nursemaid to them. They'd run her ragged while they lay around whining like a bunch of candy-asses on holiday. Harold was the worst one of all of them. He'd make Momma crazy by putting his thermometer into a hot cup of coffee, scaring the living piss out of her. Here she was scrubbing bedpans to save her son's lungs and he's playing tricks on her.

Anyway, Jessie paid no attention to old Harold, 'cause she had her sights set on Larry Easton. So naturally, Harold was jealous, which was good for him. Taste of his own medicine.

So finally one night Harold can't take it anymore, and he drags his sickly self up into the attic of that musty old cabin. Now, Harold knew a thing or two about electricity which he mostly learned from Pa, who had a job installing hand-crank phones for a while before he met Momma. And knowing a few things about the trade, Harold crawls up there, swatting spiderwebs and almost falling through the ceiling with his flashlight and some clippers and tape, and all the while he's trying to stifle his coughing 'cause it's nighttime and everybody's sleeping and he doesn't want to wake anybody up, and finally he finds the right wires and what he does is he puts a kind of crude wiretap on the phone line so he can listen in to Larry and Jessie's phone conversation when she calls in the morning like she always does.

So the sun comes up and poor Momma's running around scared out of her mind because Harold's nowhere to be found. He's still up in the attic waiting for the phone to ring. And when it finally does ring and Larry and Jessie start talking their love chatter of sweetums and blossom bottom coos, old Harold is up there with a hankie stuffed in his mouth, taking notes so he can remember all the stupid things Larry says to Jessie. And then finally Larry says he's got to get off the phone because Miss Hannah is worried about Harold because he disappeared, and that's when Jessie says, "Good. I hope that dumb old Harold Nixon wandered off into the woods and strangled up both his lungs." And that's it.

They hang up, and Momma calls down to the hospital to be on the lookout for Harold 'cause he's gone and she's worried sick, but that's when Harold drops down out of the attic and lands with a thud on the cabin floor. He's smiling and looks like he's got that edge back, like he's the favorite son again, like he owns all of Arizona and everybody in it.

Later that night is when he coos to Larry Easton from his cot across the porch. He coos all the lovey-dovey shit he overheard on the phone until Larry, so embarrassed he looks like he might soil his pajamas, shouts, "Shut up, Harold Nixon, before I beat your ass," but everyone knows Harold could take Larry in a fight any day. And then Momma comes running to say, "Boys boys, settle down now." And from under his sheets, Harold coughs lightly once and smiles, knowing that Larry Easton ain't never going to call that Jessie Lynch up again. Another victory.

And then Harold rolls over, facing Dick, and he says, "Someday, Dickie, I'm gonna tell you all my secrets. Make you into a real Nixon." Well, it isn't an exaggeration to say that young RN lay awake there nearly the whole night trying to decide if he really wanted to know all of Harold's secrets or not. He gave up thinking about it sometime near dawn when Harold's wheezing breaths finally lulled him to sleep.

Donut Joy

Besides drinking enough to drown more than one liver, Ray also smoked his fair share of dope over the years. Sometimes when he was trying to kick booze, he'd smoke whole coffee cans full of the stuff in a few days or a week. He'd sit out in the garage smoking away all night, his reward for a good day at the typewriter. He was usually on a one-joint-for-every-three-cigarettes ratio out there in the garage amid the lawn furniture and garden tools and broken telephones and all the other crap he had already collected in these lives he'd lived. He'd draw the smoke into his lungs, hold it just long enough to feel his brain tingle, then let it out slowly, savoring the taste and smell of his own exhale. In A.A. they said you weren't supposed to substitute one addiction for another, but as far as Ray was concerned, whatever kept him from drinking was okay.

Usually Ray smoked alone, but sometimes his friend Samuel would sit out in the garage with him. The two of them would smoke pot like a couple of delinquent teenagers stealing away under a porch or something. They'd be out there huddled together in the cold, sharing a homemade pipe without a screen, coughing and wheezing and laughing until way past midnight.

When they got the munchies, Ray and Samuel would make themselves a late night snack of steak with grilled onions, potato chips, and grape juice in long stem wine glasses. They'd eat, listen to Ella Fitzgerald records and giggle till morning.

One time, before Ray and Peggy split up for good, Samuel came around with a dime bag of red bud and he and Ray lit up in Samuel's Oldsmobile while they drove into town. Ray was sort of on and off the wagon then, but had yet to officially declare himself diseased. That didn't come until after his marriage was in complete ruin. Samuel was still drinking plenty in those days, but instead of taking Ray to Austin's Tavern, Samuel tooled his big Olds into the parking lot of Ray's second favorite haunt, the Donut Joy.

To Ray there was nothing quite so exquisite as the soft creamy filling of an iced long john or the crunchy delight of one of those peanut covered things. A tumbler full of whiskey was the best thing this earth had to offer, but Ray could honestly say he had never met a donut he didn't like. There was one specialty donut they carried there at the Donut Joy in town that Samuel called the black triangle. It was powdered and filled with chocolate cream and covered with sprinkles. Samuel said eating it was like performing cunnilingus.

On this particular evening Ray and Samuel were stoned to bejeezus when they arrived at the great wall of donuts. The donuts glistened under the humming florescent bulbs in the Donut Joy. The donuts spoke to Ray as he and Samuel weaved through the door and stood there swaying like devout spiritual men who had just reached the destination of their pilgrimage.

Samuel ordered without thinking, without contemplation of any sort. "Black triangle," he said. Then he explained to the donut man what he meant by this. "The one with the sprinkles, right there." He pointed to where the black triangles sat under their special glass case, separate from the regular donuts.

Ray was not so quick to choose. In fact, the selection process consumed him. He carefully looked over all fifty-two varieties, imagined the flavor of each donut in his mind, smacked his tongue against the roof of his mouth, tasting the lingering memories of glazed and powdered sugar. Then when he'd imagined them all, his plan was to review his choices, narrow the field, and go over them once more. Still, he'd have to pick a dozen or so. One or two or even a half dozen would never be enough.

So Ray stood there staring at the donut wall, imagining flavors, salivating, contemplating his options while Samuel curled his tongue and licked the frosting out of his black triangle slowly, deliberately, methodically. After a while, the donut man behind the counter sighed, wiped the underside of the sneeze guard, and said to Ray, "Let me know when you decide." He walked away, leaving Ray to scan the wall again as Samuel finished up the last few bites of his black triangle. Samuel licked his fingers, wiped his chin with a napkin and turned to Ray, whose eyes were sweeping the wall for a third time, trying to pick his final twelve.

That's when Samuel saw the tears in Ray's soft glassy eyes. Real tears. Not yawning tears or bloodshot stoner tears. No, these were real crying tears. Samuel put his hand on Ray's shoulder. "Are you okay, buddy?" he asked.

Ray sniffed. "It's just so damn hard to choose," he said. "I can't make up my mind. I can't decide." He wiped a tear away and said, "You order for me, will you, Samuel?"

Samuel smiled, "Sure, doughboy. You go sit down. I'll order."

Ray shook his head.

Samuel said, "Hey, they're just donuts, man. Right?"

"Yeah, right. Just donuts," Ray said.

But they weren't just donuts. There was more to it than that. Much more. One winter when Ray was up in Vermont teaching a writing course, he used to stock up on donuts in the cafeteria. He'd stuff his pockets full of donuts and shuffle off in the snow to his dorm room where he'd wrap them in Kleenex and stack the donuts behind the books on his shelf. He tried to be discrete about it. He didn't think anyone saw him, but it was an obsession. He had to do it, and if he got caught, so be it. A donut, even a stale one, was worth a little embarrassment in a time of need.

The first time Ray talked to Peggy was over a double choc-olate cake donut at the five and dime in Yakima where she worked the soda counter. Some years later when she had been reading up on dream theories, Peggy told Ray that his hoarding of donuts might have some psychological implication, like he was afraid of not having enough of something in his life, so he was filling the void with deep fried dough and jelly and powdered sugar. But there was more to it than that.

It was true that Ray cried that night at the Donut Joy with Samuel because he couldn't narrow his choices down to a measly dozen. He hadn't lied about that. But the tears came from some-where else too. They weren't just tears of indecision. Truth was, he felt the tears welling up in their ducts before he even finished the first cut of his donut auditions. It was when his eyes panned the bottom rack of donuts and his mind's tongue tasted the co-conut custard that he knew he was in trouble.

Dope can do that to you sometimes. Dope and donuts was an even deadlier combination. Together they could bring on a kind of dangerous nostalgia—not for days gone by, but for days that never were. And having dope and a dozen of the right donuts in the same night was like having love and marriage in the same lifetime. Too good to be true. Something was bound to go wrong—sooner or later your car would be repossessed, your land-lord would evict you, your plump blond neighbor would make an unavoidable pass at you, you'd turn into a drunk, you'd falsely accuse your wife of sleeping with a car salesman, you'd throw an ashtray at the dog, and eventually the wife you thought you'd love forever would change the locks and you wouldn't be able to get into your own house ever again. This is what Ray was thinking as he licked the imaginary coconut cream from the corners of his mouth. This is why he cried.

Ray watched the donuts watching him. They saw him for what he was, these donuts—a sad, fat poet sitting at a desk scrib-bling away, writing down the deeds of a lifetime, looking out a window now and again to watch the sea roll in. Ray wished he could get down on his knees here in front of the great wall of donuts and offer his confession, beg for the forgiveness he knew he did not deserve. He wished he could tell the donuts of all the wrongs he'd done in this life, all the harm he'd caused.

Most of all Ray wished he could take it all back. Everything he'd ever done to hurt Peggy and Julia and all the other fools who'd crossed his drunken path over the years. He wished he could take back the poems more than anything. All those private facts drudged up and passed off as fiction and all those fictions masquerading as fact—the words that catalogued their lives in such a way as to make him forget how things really happened. The poems obliterated and magnified his life at the same time. He had made a myth of himself, an invisible man. He was the donut hole, just a mouthful of air where sugar and dough should have been. He had done this to himself and to his family in the name of art— reduced the whole lot of them to reference points in an index of poem titles and first lines.

Ray didn't deserve donut joy and he knew it, so he cried, and then he told Samuel to keep the dozen donuts he'd bought for Ray. Said he'd lost his appetite, though it wasn't true. "Take me home," Ray said. And after Samuel pulled out of Ray's driveway, the sad fat poet went into his house to find the place turned upside down. Peggy had already cleared out and was gone. Maybe for good this time.

Every room showed the familiar signs of an abrupt departure— the mad rushing about that left the remains of their marriage scattered and the matted shag carpet. There was no note, no message. And there was nothing in the liquor cabinet to drink and nothing in the fridge to eat but a sad green bowl of week-old Jello. But Ray didn't cry anymore that night. He knew that but for a closing chapter or two, his first life was finally ending, and any day now, a new one might begin.

Footnote

Okay. So here's how Heroic Harold finally croaked.

It was a few days before Hannah's birthday. And it was going to be the first time the whole Nixon clan would spend the day together since Harold and Hannah had given up on the promise of Arizona and moved back to Whittier for good. Harold in his infinite generosity and wisdom decided Hannah deserved an electric mixer for her birthday, but by this time he was so fucked up with the TB. that he couldn't drive anymore. So he asked Dick to take him to the city to get the mixer. Dick, the kindly and obliging little brother, obliged as always.

In the truck on the way into L.A. they talked about nothing most of the way—baseball, mosquitoes, the way the truck was running. They also tried to outfart each other. Dick could fart with the best of them, but naturally, he was no match for Harold. With Harold it was like he was forcing all that gunk in his lungs out through his ass.

After blowing a particularly grand fart, Harold laughed and then calmly said, "Did I ever tell you how I got TB?"

Dick was surprised by the question. Harold usually pretended he wasn't even sick, and he hardly ever talked about it. Dick said, "I didn't know that you actually knew how you got it."

"It was when I went off to that Bible school in Mount Herman," Harold began.

"I remember," said Dick, "the one Pa wouldn't send me to."

"That's right," Harold said. "That's the one. Consider yourself lucky, Dick. All we ever did all day was read Scripture and get instruction in how to prepare for the Second Coming. They'd wake us up at about five o'clock in the morning and drag our butts into the shower room. I swear the water was thirty-five degrees. Then they'd make us walk half a mile to the meeting hall for a lousy breakfast of soggy toast and cold tea. There'd be icicles hanging from my hair by the time I got there."

"So that's how you got sick, huh?"

"Yeah, I already had a raging case of it by the time I got home that spring. I guess you were too young to remember."

"Is that why Pa didn't send me there?"

Harold swatted a mosquito on his arm. Dick noticed Harold's skin had a yellow tint to it. "Don't say nothing to Pa about the Bible school. To this day, I'm sure he thinks it's his fault I got TB."

"His fault?"

"Yeah. I didn't want to go to that place. He made me go."

"Ain't that funny," Dick said. "I wanted to go and you didn't. You're the one that gets to go and then it ends up making you sick."

"Pa probably sent me because he liked me better," Harold said with a crusty laugh. "And maybe because he figured you didn't really need to be prepared for the Second Coming as much as I did."

"What do you mean by that?"

"Relax, little brother, I just mean you're going to be ready when it happens. You don't need no Scripture readings or five A.M. showers. You've been getting ready for the Second Coming since the day you were born."

On the way back from buying the mixer in L.A., Harold was tired, so he lay down in the back of the truck and slept. He bounced around a lot in the flat bed as they made their way over the dusty roads. And all the way home, Dick thought he could almost hear Harold wheezing back there, but of course, that would have been impossible. The electric mixer sat in the passenger seat beside Dick. He held it down when the truck hit big bumps, and then he'd glance in the rearview mirror to see if maybe Harold had been bounced out of the truck into a ditch or something. Somehow Harold slept through it all.

When they got home, Harold stumbled awkwardly into the house and went back to sleep on the sofa. Dick took the mixer to his room to wrap it up and hide it under his bed.

The next day, Dick went off to his classes at Whittier High. In history class, while Mr. Oberhoffer was oversimplifying the causes of the Great Depression and most of the students were thinking about sex or the upcoming dance or a new play the coach wanted them to learn, Dick was thinking about how his whole life had been totally fucked up by Harold. Dick had just gotten his acceptance letter from Duke University, but naturally, there wasn't enough money left to pay the tuition, on account of Harold's doctor bills. Dick would be going to Whittier College for at least two years with all the rest of the yokel Quaker dopes.

Mr. Oberhoffer said something about the bull market, and the girl behind Dick poked him in the back. She wanted him to pass a note up to the boy in the next row. Dick obliged.

That was when Principal Klindschmidt came into the classroom, walked right up to Dick's desk, and escorted him out into the hall.

The principal closed the classroom door, placed his hands on Dick's shoulders, and said, "Your mother called, son. She wants you to come home. Your brother has died."

So that's how it finally happened. Harold was gone. And for the first time Dick saw that Harold was nobody. Had always been nobody. Always would be nobody. Just Richard Nixon's older brother—the one who died of TB. A footnote. A sack of phlegmy lungs, brittle bones, and yellow skin. And then finally, ashes. Dust.

• • •

As for the electric mixer, Dick never gave it to Hannah. After Harold's funeral, Dick took the mixer out behind the grocery store and tried to smash it into very small pieces with a baseball bat. He pounded away at it, imagining shards and metal shrapnel leaping into the air and applauding him as he raised his bat again and again. The wooden bat splintered, and he managed to dent and scratch the mixer, but in the end, he was unable to kill it.

Sante Fe

The Sante Fe line carried citrus fruit to the heartland. It chugged right by Dick's bedroom window. Sometimes, late at night, he'd climb out of bed and sit by the window and listen for the train. He'd try to predict how long it would be before the next one would come. He'd count slowly and deliberately to prove his prediction right. In the empty bed across the room, the ghost of Harold would shudder with night sweats whenever Dick threw open the window sash to listen.

Citrus. That was what California had to offer the nation—the tart pucker of sour lemons. The train cars rattled and lumbered off into the early morning, their gift from the West on board, bouncing in crates in every car all down the line.

Dick watched the train and imagined the stacks of oranges, lemons, and limes in the boxcars. In bed, Harold's ghost shivered and kicked at his blankets, moaning in harmony with Pa in the next room, who snorted and called out in his sleep every time a train started up the hill toward their house. Pa and Harold were speaking a dream language, carrying on a forbidden conversation in which Dick would never be welcome.

Dick imagined himself a conductor on the Sante Fe line, shoveling coal, barking commands, blowing his big whistle—on his way to somewhere far from Whittier, far from Yorba Linda, far from Prescott even. East of everything. Somewhere else.

He imagined great piles of money and crowds of people. The beautiful calves of women in silk skirts. The strong, clean jaws of men who only had to shave once a day. The lights hanging from poles and wires above the city streets. Streetcar motormen who called out the stops. The smell of popcorn in the movie theaters. Alley cats who lived on garbage and mice but were perfectly happy to do so.

In the cities out east children played games of stickball in the street, and their giggles echoed off the brick pavement. Dick imagined himself umpiring a street game, calling the balls and strikes, making sure the sides were even, the game fair.

In this way he was elsewhere—outside himself, offering the world something bigger than California's sour lemons—talking his own night language to a distant audience that would someday hang on his every word. *Strike three, yer out!* he'd yell. And the whole street would explode. A roaring crowd of spectators lined up on the sidewalks would leap to its feet, cheers of approval for the winners ringing out up and down the block.

But as the train clumped out of sight, Dick sighed and climbed back into bed. If sleep came to him, it would be full of nightmares. He could only hope, as the invisible lungs of his dead brother wheezed beside him, that another train would be by soon.

Watching Vera Dance

After that first fateful, failed date, their courtship lasted two years, their engagement one and a half. Most of that time they were together on the campus at Whittier College. They'd had their first tiff about the school's policy forbidding dancing on campus. Dick was running for class president at the time when Vera said to him, "If you expect my vote, you'll do something about the oppression on this campus."

"But, Vera," Dick said, "Quakers just don't dance."

Pointing to herself, Vera said, "Well, this one does, Dick Nixon."

Dick lost the argument and promised to fight to reform the school's policy on dancing. It's what got him elected eventually. If not for Vera's advice, he would not have convinced his fellow Quaker students he was worthy of their support. His slogan was: "A vote for Dick Nixon is a vote for the dancing candidate." In truth, Dick hated dancing, didn't know the first thing about it.

When the administration legalized dancing at Whittier College, thanks to Dick's persuasive tactics, Vera dragged Dick to every dance function the school sponsored. But Vera always danced alone. In the middle of the dance floor. Surrounded by couples dancing at proper arms-length distance from each other. They spun around Vera. She was their center. Their gravity source. They watched Vera—her eyes closed, her head tilted back, her body turning in a dizzying pattern of circles, ovals, figure eights. Vera lifted her arms, waved them like a drugged bird, her head swimming on the end of its loose neck. Her shoulders were inside the rhythm, joined with it, coursing into it.

Vera smiled when the rhythm changed. Without being aware of it, the other dancers changed direction at Vera's silent command. They shifted gears, altered position. She led, they followed.

Vera danced with everyone. She had dozens of partners at once. Somehow she was in tune with all of their movements, connected to them like the spheres in heaven dancing to their perfect music. Vera orchestrated, choreographed. She designed new moves no one had ever seen before. She had new knowledge. She was everyone's perfect dance partner. This is why she danced alone—so that she could dance with everyone.

From a quiet corner, sipping punch, Dick Nixon, the "dancing candidate," watched his beautiful date, Vera Louise, as she caressed the crowd. Dick spilled a dribble of the red punch on his sport coat. The same klutz he was in high school. The same kid who was called the team punching bag by the Whittier High football coach.

Watching Vera dance as he tried to wipe the red stain from his sport coat, he wanted to believe she was perfect for him, but Vera was a rainbow gal. That's why he wanted to get in her panties so bad, of course, but he wouldn't have know what to do with all that color. Things were white or they were black; gray wasn't even in his vocabulary, let alone the whole prism of rainbow hues. Vera was a dreamer. A beautiful fool.

They were to be married at the Friends church in Whittier as soon as Dick finished up his law degree at Duke. But with Dick at Duke sitting on his iron butt, trying to study law and imagining old Vera dancing her sloppy wet crotch all over campus back at Whittier College, the engagement was doomed from the start. Everyone knew this of course. Everyone except dumb Dick who wrote her love letters daily, professing his respectable intentions and preparing her for the life she would live as Mrs. Richard Milhous Nixon. "You're going to be married to a lawyer," he wrote, "so you'll have to be versed in the matters of the law." And then page after page of some Supreme Court decision that only he cared about. Vera rarely finished the letters.

After a while, Vera stopped wearing the engagement ring. And eventually, she wrote him to break it off. She said she was going with Bill Adams. "He's more reckless and silly than you," she wrote. "And he knows how to dance." She and Bill Adams were discussing marriage, she told Dick in the letter's P.S. just so he'd know for sure it was really over. When Dick got her letter, he called Vera long distance and said, "If I never talk to you again, it'll be too soon." He hung up before she could respond and that was that.

But a few days later, another letter arrived in Vera's mailbox. It said basically, "This is the last time I'm ever going to write to you. Good riddance."

But it wasn't the last time. In less than a week, another letter came. In it, Dick apologized for his behavior. He wrote, "I wish I could keep from losing my temper. I remember the first time I took you out. After I left you that night, a train whistle sounded in the distance, and I looked up and there were the pointy stars sparkling out their promises in all directions. I love you, Vera Louise. And I will love you always. But this is goodbye."

It wasn't goodbye, though, because he wrote again to say, "I realize I blew it with you and don't think I'm trying to get you back because I know you are happier now with Bill Adams. I'm being sentimental but I mean it when I say you meant more to me than my own meager existence. When I gaze out the window above my desk I know that there was never a better woman than Vera Louise Parker." Between writing these lines at the desk in his dorm room, Dick Nixon curled up in a ball on his bed with stomach cramps, and he shiver-weeped. Vera had poisoned him forever. "May I please have an invitation to your wedding?" he wrote. "I want to witness your happy day. With love, Richard."

For six months while Vera Louise and Bill Adams planned their wedding, the letters from Dick kept coming. And coming.

In one he professed his undying love. In the next he told her she was scum. In almost all of them, he vowed never to write to her again. And in more than a few he repeated his request for a wedding invitation.

Vera never responded to the letters except once, about a month before her wedding to Bill Adams when she wrote to say, "Please, please, please stop sending me letters. It's over."

But Dick kept writing up until just a few days before Vera's wedding, to which he had not been invited. In his last letter, he wrote this: "Finally I have become wise. And while I regret my foolishness, I do not regret the feelings I've had for you these last few years. Vera, you are a dancer. You're everyone's partner and no one's at the same time. If we would have married, I'd forever be the klutzy husband standing in the corner wiping a juice stain off his jacket. I'd never be able to get on the dance floor with you. It would violate who you are. It would stiffen your shoulders, make you stoop, confuse your rhythm. In short, it would make you a Nixon. I shall always remember the kindness, the beauty, the loveliness that was, that is, and shall forever be Vera Louise. Your friend, Dick."

On the day Vera Louise Parker became Mrs. William Adams in Whittier, California, Dick Nixon, back in the bathroom of his dormitory at Duke, could be heard vomiting thirteen times.

Dick assured himself that Vera Louise was a cunt. She was the San Andreas Fault, he told himself, and sooner or later, the entire state of California would be swallowed up into her crack.

He missed all his classes the following week. On the cold, hard tile floor in his room he sat with his legs crossed, rocking back and forth and humming some strange indistinguishable song to himself. There was no particular melody to it. It had no rhythmic pattern, no beginning, and no end. All week long he hummed and rocked like that. All week, with his eyes closed. Sometimes the hum was quiet, barely audible. Sometimes it turned into a roaring chant. Sometimes it was fast, sometimes slow. But all the while he kept up that steady rocking. The same pace, the same motion. All week long.

Old Habits

The ashtray lies between them on the kitchen table, overflowing with brown-corked butts, and smoldering. Ray and Peggy sit at opposite ends of the table, orbiting the ashtray like repulsive magnetic poles, the ashtray their equator.

Ray takes a drag off his cigarette. Sucks the smoke as deep as he can, his lungs filling with the warmth. Peggy watches him. He hopes he looks like Bogart or John Wayne. He suspects she knows he is hoping this. Being married to a poet gives a woman certain keen abilities—a kind of built-in shit detector.

The table, like the ashtray and everything else in the kitchen, reeks of Peggy's new life. There's a cheap clean vinyl smell to the room, which Ray happily violates by blowing casual smoke rings up toward the light hanging above the table. Peggy lives here now, has for some time. She uses this ashtray every day, no doubt. Eats breakfast off this marble-gray table, its wobbly chrome legs supporting runny eggs and coffee.

Ray tries to remember his first date with Peggy, but nothing comes to him. Then he recalls glimpses of their first meeting—he sees glazed donuts and Peggy's five-and-dime waitress outfit, her thin legs, a walk on the outskirts of town by the sawmill where his father worked, the kiss goodnight.

For an instant, Ray contemplates smashing the ashtray against the wall. He imagines the glass shards flying back at them in

slow motion and wonders if the gesture would look like a last
ditch effort to save something or an act meant to convey finality?
He's not sure which so he just takes another drag off his cigarette, avoiding Peggy's gaze. He flicks ashes off the end of his cigarette. Outside he can hear the rain dripping off a clogged gutter.
Soon Ray will stub out his last cigarette and leave this kitchen
for good.

Peggy massages the indentation in her ring finger where her
wedding band used to be. Ray watches those long slender fingers
of hers. The gesture is ever-so-gentle, the perfect touch, so pained,
so thoughtful—this much she concedes and he is grateful. Ray
wonders if she'll mention the rain outside, rely on it as a metaphor
of sorts. He would do it himself, but this would be stealing her
lines. He takes a last drag, stubs the butt, and then gets up, almost
knocking his chair over on the linoleum.

Ray walks across the room to the sink, turns the faucet handle
and runs the water for no particular reason other than he wants to
see how things work in this new kitchen of Peggy's. There's a
window above the sink, something she always wanted. Ray looks
out at the yard, trying to imagine what Peggy thinks about when
she stands here washing dishes. The rain is not letting up. Before
long the entire yard will be one big pond, and Ray will have to
canoe his way out of this place.

Today it is too late, but tomorrow if the rain clears, he'll go
for a walk and tip his hat to lovely ladies in skirts and heels. He'll
say "Good afternoon" to total strangers. But no matter what he
does tomorrow or the next day or the day after, a part of him will
always be here at this window, watching the rain fall, wondering
if he's playing his role well.

Peggy offers this: "Maybe it's not too late to do something."
The words are warm smoke in his chest, nicotine in his veins,
deadly but oh-so-soothing. A consolation prize.

He watches her as she massages her temples. Another habit of
hers. He grinds his teeth and turns back to the window. He
watches the rain, pulls another cigarette out of its pack, lights it,
and then holds the burning match out between thumb and fore-

finger. He stares at it a moment, then blows it out and looks at the sizzle of the gray tip as the smoke rises around him.

He can't stand at this window forever. This thing has to end at the table. Face to face. So he sits. Peggy reaches across the table. He thinks she's reaching for his hand, but she motions for his cigarette. She wants a drag, she says. His hand crosses the equator. Their fingers touch. The cigarette changes hands. She drags, he watches. The smoke gets in her eye, and it tears. She hands the cigarette back.

When she cries, it comes in gentle heaves. He waits, doesn't say anything. The thing to do now is ride it out. He hopes the rain stops soon so he can make a clean exit, turning his collar to the damp and walking off with her still crying at the table. He hopes that's how it ends. He also hopes tomorrow he'll have a new part to play.

Requests from the King

September 9, 1969

TO: H. R. Haldeman
FROM: The President
RE: Miscellaneous Requests

I have an uneasy feeling that many of the items that I send out for action are disregarded when any staff member just reaches a conclusion that it is unreasonable or unattainable. In the future, I want you to keep a checklist of everything I order and I want you to indicate what action has been taken. Now, having said that, there are a number of items I would like you to attend to ASAP. They follow in no particular order, that is to say they are not prioritized here, as I am trusting you to address all of them concurrently and expediently.

Item: In talking with the GSA Director with regard to RN's room, what would be most desirable is an end table like the one on the right side of the bed which will accommodate *two* Dictaphones as well as a telephone. RN has to use one Dictaphone for current matters and another for memoranda for the file which he will not want transcribed at this time. In addition, the table which is presently in the room does not allow enough room for RN to get his knees under it.

Item: Would you please give RN a report on the official picture of the President? As you will recall, the picture hanging in the Defense Department is much too severe. RN does not look that severe in person. If that is the picture which has been selected for the White House, I want it changed.

Item: When the Oval Office is redone RN would like to have a coffee table in front of the fireplace replaced by one that does not block his view of the fireplace from the desk. Also, pending the decisions in regards to the Oval Office and the West Wing renovations, RN would like something done immediately with regard to the George Washington painting over the fireplace. It should either be moved up or the clock should be moved out.

Item: The silver Parker pen that was given to RN on Election Day, November 5, 1968, is such a good one that he would like to get another one exactly like it as a spare. Will you check it out and arrange for a purchase.

Item: RN noticed that California red wine was served at last night's dinner. It is his standing instruction that California wine is never to be served at State Dinners—especially those for Europeans. Also, on the subject of wine, would you please have the Bordeaux checked. We seem to have a lot of '66 Bordeaux on hand, which is one of the poor years. See if you can trade it for some '59, an excellent year.

Item: In the area of food, I feel that the portions of meat (specifically the huge steaks) served on the *Sequoia,* at Camp David, etc. are too large and I would like the size cut down substantially. Speak to Rose Mary and find out who is responsible.

Question: What is the situation with regard to the horrible modern art in some of our embassies? I realize we can't censor the stuff, but I would like a report as to what embassies have some of these atrocious objects. I don't mind if an Ambassador likes modern art provided he is doing a good job in other respects. But I don't want our embassies to be unrepresentative of America.

Item: RN would like you to have a check made on the chairs in the Cabinet Room. These chairs, because of their style, are very uncomfortable. For one thing they do not leave enough legroom beneath the table, and as I have told you before, at least insofar as RN's chair is concerned, it is stiff and hard and pretty uncomfortable after one of those god-awful meetings goes as long as an hour or more.

Item: While on a tour of Pennsylvania Avenue last week, I saw that the signs currently marked "Government Building" need to be taken down and replaced with more attractive signs. They should be made with more strength and dignity. Also, RN wants the lower portion of the Capitol to be sandblasted before the Middle Easterners come.

Item: With regard to musical entertainment, I am somewhat above average because I know something about music and frankly, last night I was pretty bored. In the future, I do not want anybody with esoteric tastes to have anything to do with the selection of the musical entertainment.

Item: Regarding the key to the refrigerator. It is ridiculous to have a medallion of JFK on the key to President Nixon's refrigerator. I believe an RMN medallion should be on the keys.

I fully expect these items to be addressed promptly. If anyone feels there is any reason to consider any of the above "unreasonable" I want to know about it. Please send me a memo regarding your progress on these items before our Wednesday morning meeting.

According to Manolo

Early one morning in 1970, you see I am a light sleeper, and on this morning I awoke, it's part of my job to be a light sleeper, and I awoke to the sound of Rachmaninoff's Second Piano Concerto coming from the Lincoln Sitting Room. It was about 4:00 A.M. Who knows why a person would listen to piano music at all hours of the night, but it was not uncommon for the President to wake and remove himself to the Lincoln Room to listen to his records. When he did this, I would bring him coffee or tea. Sometimes I would sit with him. We would talk, he would ask me about myself and tell me his troubles, which I often did not understand. Other times we would just sit and listen to the music.

This particular morning, the President was standing at his window looking out at the Washington Monument. I stared at it with him for a while and I commented on how I thought it was very beautiful. The President said the Lincoln Memorial was actually much more beautiful. He said it was the most beautiful sight in all of Washington at night. I confessed I had never seen it. My duties as the President's personal valet did not allow me to do much sight-seeing at night.

That's when the President said, "Get your coat, Manolo, we'll go see it now."

He did not even tell the security men or the reporters or Mrs. Nixon that we were going. We just got our coats and left.

When we arrived, we discovered a group of young people who were college students. They had long hair and were gathered on the steps of the monument. The President told me they were protesters camped out overnight, waiting for a rally that was to begin the next day.

The President walked right up to the young people and started shaking hands with them. Then he asked them where they were from and what they were studying. One girl was from California, and he told her where some good surfing was by his home in San Clemente. Then he asked the students what they thought of his press conference about Vietnam. Then he said to them, "I know that probably most of you think I'm an SOB, but I want you to know that I understand how you feel." I don't know for sure, but I think maybe the President wanted to debate the students. I think he wanted to fight it out with them right there on the steps of the Lincoln Memorial. But the students were so shocked to be standing there with the President that they were sort of dumbfounded. They didn't respond at all to his questions about the war even though they were there to protest the war. He had managed to silence them by his very presence.

The President explained that he was a Quaker and said that made him a pacifist. He talked about traveling to far-off lands and about clean air and crime and matters of the spirit. He told them many things about his beliefs. He told them, "Something that is completely clean and sterile can be without spirit." And he talked to them about their colleges' football teams and how they were doing that year. I don't remember all the other details, but he spoke at them until the sun came up.

One of the students asked for his photograph, and so I took the camera and snapped a picture of the President with his arm around the student's shoulder. The student asked the President what he was going to have for breakfast when he got back to the White House. The President said he'd be having Grape-Nuts as he did every morning. That was the same student, I think, who befriended the President some years later. If I'm not mistaken, that's the young man. He used to come up to the house at San

Clemente from time to time. I don't remember his name now, but they became quite close.

As we walked down the steps in the early sunlight, many more students were climbing up over the Washington Monument and heading down toward the Lincoln Memorial to see the President. He tried to shake the hands of those people nearest to him. One young woman yelled out, "I hope you know we're prepared to die for our beliefs." The President made his way over to the girl and shook her hand and said, "I just hope our opposition doesn't turn into blind hatred."

That's all I remember, but it is my favorite memory about the President. I was Mr. Richard Nixon's personal valet for over fifteen years—from the White House to San Clemente—and this is the event I always think of first when someone asks me to describe the President.

Luck

Dick lights his cigar, shakes out the match, puts his ante into the pot, and says, "Did I ever tell you two about the time I debated those kids up at the Lincoln Memorial?"

Ray and I both nod, fanning our cards out. "Yes, Dick. We've heard that one."

"How about the time I broke up the fight between the motorists?" he says, chewing on the already soggy tip of his cigar.

We've heard the motorist story too, of course, but Ray shoots me a look that says, Let him tell it, so I just ask for three new cards and don't say anything.

Dick deals. My cards suck. Dick starts his story: "So we're sitting at a complete standstill in this major D.C. traffic jam. I got Chuck Colson in the backseat with me and some Secret Service pud up in front driving. Colson points out the window and says, 'Hey, no wonder. There's an accident up there. And look, there's two guys going at it.' Sure enough, I take a look out the window and there's two guys in the middle of the highway, standing alongside the wreck, and they're squaring off, pointing in each other's faces, yelling, the whole bit."

I fold my cards and say, "So then what happened, Dick?" even though I know the whole story by heart. Ray drops a blue chip into the pot, Dick raises him.

"Well," says Dick, "I got right out of that car and walked up to those two bastards and pulled them apart and told them to settle their differences in a more appropriate place because the president of the United States of America didn't enjoy being stuck in a fucking traffic jam."

"Call," says Ray. "What do you got?"

"Aces over nines," says Dick spreading his cards out on the table.

"Beats me," Ray says. "You got some streak going tonight, Dick. What did you do, eat an extra bowl of Wheaties this morning?" The truth is Dick always seems to have a streak going when we play cards together.

"Playing cards," Dick says, "is like playing the piano. You've got to know what note comes next or else the whole thing falls apart. It's a matter of instinct. Like when I broke up that fight on the highway. How did I know one of those two assholes didn't have a gun or a knife or something? Just instinct. I took one look at them and I said to myself, 'This is a problem RN can solve.' And so I solved it. When I got back to the car, Colson and the Secret Service guy were just sitting there with their mouths hanging open. I'd taken the poor bastards by surprise. They were so shocked they hadn't even chased after me or anything. You should have seen the looks on their faces."

"When you got back in the car, what did you say to them?" Ray offers.

"Nothing. I just looked at them and went, 'What? What did I do that was so strange?'"

Ray and I conjure up the expected laughter and shake our heads.

My deal. I choose a seven-card, no-peek game. When I deal the cards, Ray lets his fall into a kind of haphazard, messy pile. The pile is chaotic, formless—little disasters are hiding in there somewhere, waiting to happen. Dick can barely suppress the urge to peek at his cards, but he manages to control himself by arranging his cards into a neat row. Each card hangs over the edge of the card next to it by about a centimeter, and each is perfectly aligned with its neighbors. He stares at the cards as if trying to read through their backs. Occasionally, he rearranges the order of his cards, following some premonition or instinct.

After I've dealt, I find myself spreading my cards in a kind of circular, almost floral arrangement. The contrast in the way we set up our cards is so comical I wish I had a camera so I could capture the absurdity of it.

For a while I lose track of the game and play it like a half-conscious driver behind the wheel of a big comfortable car, making his way down a road he's driven a thousand times before. I'm on autopilot, and the cards play themselves. My stack of chips shrinks, as does Ray's. Dick's winning again, as usual. And he's shooting the bull the whole time, telling us his stories. Ray's laughing a kind of conspiratorial laugh that bounces off the ceiling and comes back at me when I least expect it.

Dick tells about Abe Lincoln at Gettysburg, Ray tells about Chekhov. Ray says Chekhov died of TB. The irony isn't lost on any of us. Dick says, "You ought to write a biography or a poem or something."

"You think that's something," Ray says. "Listen to this." And then he tells us about how he and Beth used to drive up and down the coast looking for bingo games at churches and VFW halls. They'd cheat just to see if the old ladies would catch them. It was something they did for fun when they first found out he had cancer.

Soon enough we forget we're even playing cards and the stories just keep coming. Dick's got practically all of our money now anyway, so he's happy to put the game on hold. "Did I ever tell you about the Orthogonians?" he asks. And this is, surprisingly enough, a story we *haven't* heard yet.

"It was when I was at Whittier College. I joined this fraternal club called the Orthogonians. Actually, I was one of the founders. I came up with the name, the symbols. I even wrote the slogans."

"What were the symbols?" Ray wants to know.

"A square, which stood for a well-rounded life of 'brains, brawn, beans, and bowels.' And a boar's head."

"And was there a motto?" I ask, snickering at the casual way Dick says bowels.

"Stamp out evil," Dick says. "That was the motto."

Ray and I are trying our best to contain ourselves because Dick looks as if he's getting to a serious point of some sort. He says, "Anyway, the whole thing got out of control. It was almost all football players in the club and they decided we needed an initiation ritual. And even though I was a founder of the damn club, they made me go through the initiation."

"What did they do to you?" I ask.

"The bastards stripped me down to my birthday suit in the middle of winter, made me sit on a block of ice outside for an hour, and then drove me in an open-air rumble seat out to the woods, where they made me lick the flesh of a dead dog. Raw."

"Good God," Ray says.

"God had nothing to do with it," says Dick. "I was sick for weeks."

The stories go on for hours, of course. There's the one about the winter flies hibernating in the air ducts that attacked when Ray finally paid his heat bill. And the one about the time when Dick couldn't eat before a big high school football game and then was offsides in all two of his plays. There's the father who got an erection every time he hugged his wife. And the other father who left his hearing aid at home when he went to see his son sing in the school production of *Oklahoma!* There are dreams of greatness, dreams of being an actor, a preacher, a quarterback, a farmer, a pianist, baseball commissioner. And of course, there are the missed opportunities and the ridiculous failures.

The playing cards lie limp on the green felt table, strewn amid waiting poker chips. The cigar smoke rises and the stories continue. We don't play poker together because we share a lifelong love of the game or something. Ultimately, we play because it's an excuse to swap stories. A chance for Dick to shake his jowls and tell about the time his old man gave his dog away while he was off getting his law degree. A chance for Ray to lean in and tell in his thin, airy voice about the time when he was bankrupt and a guy sued him for his dog because it was all he had. And if there's an opening, I'll tell about how my dog ran away on Thanksgiving when I was thirteen. Then we'll all laugh at our pathetic lives—Ray always laughing the hardest, that big high laugh of his filling the room, tears coming out of his eyes, and him saying. "Think of it," or "You don't say," or "Imagine that!"

Finally sometime before dawn Dick deals out a last hand of screw your neighbor and Ray says, "We're all damn lucky, you know."

I want to ask Ray what he means by this, but Dick cuts in. "Lucky my ass," he says. "You're dying and I'm a total fuckup. And this stupid putz," he says, pointing to me, "has got nothing better to do than sit around here and listen to our sorry-ass life stories because he doesn't have a life of his own."

"No," says Ray, "we're damn lucky. All of us."

Dick says, "You're cracked, cancer-for-brains."

"I'm dying," Ray says. "So what. We're all dying. The difference is I'm writing a poem about it in my head right now. That's what makes me lucky."

"Oh Jesus, here we go," Dick says, throwing up his hands, then reaching for the cards to shuffle.

"Look," Ray says to Dick, "I should have been dead from the booze long ago. You've been dead a half dozen times or more already. But we survive. We go on. We resurrect ourselves. That's luck, my friend. That's gravy. And the kid here, he's got all that to look forward to yet. I say we're three lucky sons-of-bitches."

"I think all that AA crap is going to your head," Dick says. "You sound like a damn Quaker."

I manage to say, "Dick, maybe Ray's right. Maybe we are lucky. I mean, I realize I don't have the luxury of seeing the world through your eyes, so maybe I'm being naive, but isn't it possible . . ."

Dick cuts me off. "Look, kid, one thing I definitely don't need right now is second rate philosophy from a putz like you."

"Fine," I say, passing my two of hearts to Ray.

"Ugh," he says, looking at the card. He passes it to Dick and says, "The kid's right. So I need chemotherapy. So I'm dying. But for God's sake, people pay me for my words. Think of it. And on top of that, I got a wife who loves me."

Dick turns the two over and takes a card off the deck. It's a king. He's high card again. "You also got an ex-wife who hates your guts," he says, clearing the cards and dealing the next round.

Ray sticks with his card. So does Dick. I go off the deck. It's another two, spades this time. I'm low. Ray says, "You think you're not lucky? You want to talk real suffering? I once wrote a screenplay about Dostoyevsky. Now there's a guy who suffered. Epilepsy, bankruptcy, exile. Nobody ever bought my screenplay, but you know what? That's as it should be. It's all about the suffering. And the suffering is irrelevant. That, we won't remember. What we will remember is *Crime and Punishment, The Brothers Karamazov, The Idiot.* That's what matters. That's what makes even Dostoyevsky a lucky man."

Dick clears the cards, deals another round. He shakes his head. "And I suppose I'm lucky because everyone will forget Watergate after I'm dead and remember me for my piano playing."

"Maybe," Rays says. "No way to know yet. No crystal ball, you know. One thing's for sure. You will be remembered." He turns his card over. It's a king. But Dick's got the ace.

I'm out. And it's down to the two of them now. But I'm tired and I don't feel like sticking around to see how it ends. Besides, I know how it will end. With the cards Dick's been getting all night, he can't lose. This is the way it is every time we play poker. Dick always cleans us out. It's like an unwritten rule. Sometimes I wonder if he cheats. But I know better. He doesn't have to cheat. Especially with a game like screw your neighbor. It's like playing war—pure luck. Dick can't lose.

Pianist

Dick dick dick dick. What kind of a person names his son Dick? This was what Dick thought about as the master of ceremonies introduced him. "Dick Nixon," the pompous MC said, "is of course most well known for his political life, but what many people don't realize is that he is unquestionably one of this country's most accomplished pianists." From behind the blue velvet curtain in the stage wing, Dick could see the audience nodding its approval. They loved him, the fools.

The MC droned on about Dick Nixon's greatness. Blah blah blah. "Musical genius," he said. "Wizard at the keyboard," he said. "A master of deception, playing as if he had ten hands with twenty fingers on each hand."

It was all true, of course, but frankly Dick was bored with it. Debussy, Mozart, Chopin. A bunch of fruitcakes, Dick thought. Even Bach, what a dupe. Dances, minuets, concertos. There was a time when being the greatest piano player on the planet really mattered to Dick. But now it was just so much humdrum. The adoring fans, the exclusive engagements, all of it. He could stand on his head and play chopsticks and they'd still cheer. The challenge was gone.

"It gives me great pleasure," said the MC, "to introduce a truly marvelous pianist, a wonderful man, Mr. Dick Nixon."

There it was again. That name. Dick. Maybe he should walk

out on stage, unzip his fly, and flash them his flange—let them see the real Dick Nixon. He stepped out from behind the curtain. The audience erupted in a tasteful roar. Dick paused at the edge of the stage on his way to the piano. The silly onlookers elbowed each other and pointed as if to say, There he is. That's him. That's Dick. Can you believe we're actually going to hear him play in person? He sighed and made his way to the piano bench. He wondered if Beethoven ever felt this way.

The proverbial hush fell over the peanut gallery. Dick flipped back the tails of his tux and sat. Beethoven, he thought, that's where I'll begin. His left hand fluttered over the keys effortlessly. He could feel the audience gasp, holding its collective breath, stifling its coughs and titters. The right hand swept the ivory dramatically. He was giving the people what they wanted.

There were corpuscles flowing through him that were Beethoven's. Sounds that came out of his piano reincarnated old Ludwig, that crazy deaf fuck who would have killed his own father to be great. Dick was sexing the keys, gestating the notes, birthing the sloppy, bloody mess of music that *was* the German master.

The deafness crept into Dick's ears slowly at first. A muffle, then a warp, then a cloudy, distant ether fog of soundlessness. His fingers were train wheels on a never-ending track, thrust forward by a locomotion he did not wish to control. The wheels chugged, churned, even whined a little. Someone in the first row winced. But Dick was blind now too. He pressed on, unaware that he had gone off track. California-bound, he slammed the piano into a higher gear, shoveling coal into the engine like a madman, pounding out the dissonant scales that would take him home. No melody. No rhythm. Just sheer bumpy backward motion.

The people in the audience sat aghast, mouths hanging open. But Dick chugged on. I am Dick, his fingers shouted. I am Dick. Dick dick dick dick. They named me Dick, the bastards. They named me Dick. I am Dick. Fuck you all. Fuck them too. I'll fuck you with my big dick. I'll slap this schlong onto the keys and show you what Dick is all about, you hopeless fuck-faced ding-a-lings! Dick does this. And this. And this! Dick is Frank. Dick is Hannah.

Dick is Harold. Dick is Arthur. Dick is dick. I am Dick, the dick dick dick. Take that! And that! And that. You cod-sucking, lily-ass, pretentious bastards, bitches, sons of bitches, ass wipes, and pud whackers. You don't know dick. But I'll show you. I'll show you. I'll show you. Dick dick. Dick dick dick. Lick my butt, you brain-dead shitheads! This is what I think of you. This is what I think of Beethoven. And Bach. And all the rest. They don't know dick either. Well here he is, world. Suck him dry, if you dare. But you're no match for him. You haven't got balls big enough for this dick. Eat me! I am Dick.

The last note quavered in the air. It hung there and dissipated ever so slowly. The panic in the crowd subsided. It gave way to shock, then anger. How dare he do that to Beethoven? Who does he think he is? their eyes said to one another.

Dick found himself standing at the piano. He had kicked the bench out from behind him at some point. His tuxedo jacket lay on the floor near the front of the stage, torn. His armpits were soaked with sweat. His once neatly slicked hair dangled furiously about his brow. He held his hands up to his face. When they came into focus, he saw they were still trembling. He looked down at his feet. He was barefoot. His shoes were nowhere in sight.

When they escorted Dick off the stage, they did so with great caution, as if they feared he might harm them in some way. But there was no need to worry. He was back among them now. Back here in this theater wondering what would happen next. Wondering what the reviewers would say in the morning papers. Wondering if he'd ever play piano publicly again. Wondering if it really mattered. Wondering if the ghosts in California had heard him.

Nothing

Ray never yelled at his father. Not once. Not ever. He thought about it plenty of times. Wished he'd had the balls to do it somewhere along the line. But like most sons, he kept quiet.

Growing up, Ray had seen plenty of things that gave him just cause. He had seen his old man slam his fist into automobile dashboards, plaster walls, and plenty of other places. He had heard the late-night screaming and the crying and the iron skillet hitting the kitchen floor. And he had seen the parade of floozies. Still Ray never laid into the old man. Never let him have it. Never even acknowledged that he had witnessed these things. Not even later, when he was old enough and had every right to put the old bastard in his place.

Eventually it was too late. Ray's father went catatonic in a white room, and there was nothing left to say. The words would stay where they had always been—inside some dim, frothy place Ray imagined bubbling with acids and sizzling with smoke.

The first and only time Ray went to visit his father in the hospital, he brought a recent copy of *Outdoor* magazine and a smoked salmon. The fish was wrapped in wax paper and foil, and Ray offered it up to the unblinking face of his father. A gift, a consolation. The old man didn't budge.

"It's smoked," Ray said. "Just caught it last weekend."

Nothing.

Ray sat, reached for his father's hand. It was cold. Puffy. He wanted to say, Tell me a story, Pop. Tell me about how you rode the rails when you were my age. Tell me the lie about how your grandfather fought for both sides in the Civil War. Read me something from this magazine I brought you.

Instead, Ray said, "I'm writing." Then he said, "It's going well. A poem a day." It was a lie. He was drinking mostly. It was going lousy. Everything was lousy. He wanted to say, Peggy's going to leave me. We're out of money. I'm killing myself with booze. My daughter comes home in a cop car twice a week. He wanted to say, We're bankrupt, and I keep writing the same poem over and over but I never get it right, and it's all your fault, you bastard. Look what you've done to me.

If Ray *were* writing in those days, he would have written a poem about a boy who stands at a bus stop on a Friday afternoon. The boy is waiting for his father to come home from his job at the sawmill. He waits for hours. The sky grows red, then purple, then black. Still the boy waits. But it's payday, and the boy knows better. His father won't be on the next bus. Or the one after that. A pocket full of change means a bladder full of beer. The boy's father might not be back till morning, or he might not be back till Sunday night, or he might not be back at all. The air grows cold. The boy wraps his arms around himself and continues to wait. He'll stay here all night if he has to. There's a point to be made. And he's going to make it without saying a word.

If Ray wrote such a poem, he'd like to give it to his father. Or maybe he'd read it out loud to him here in this sterile hospital room. He could, of course, just tell the story to his father. It need not have rhythm and metaphor to make its point.

But Ray didn't say much of anything the afternoon of his first and only visit to his father's catatonic white room. What would have been the point of dragging everything out of the acid now? In the end, a man does what he does because he's a genetic victim, a testosterone-driven fool trapped in an inadequate and hopeless disguise. Ray knew that better than anyone, so he didn't say anything. And his old man didn't say anything. They just sat and stared together at the white wall. At nothing. Every few minutes Ray looked over at his father to see if he'd snapped out of it. Nothing.

An odd calm came over Ray eventually. Not a pleasant calm. A kind of full emptiness. He knew he was supposed to feel something, and he did, in fact, feel lots of things. But finally he was resigned to let the feelings alone. They hadn't stopped festering. It's just that he knew now that they weren't going anywhere— these things he felt. He was stuck with them, and that was that.

He got up and walked to the window. There was nothing out there. A gray horizon line and a fence. Asphalt. Maybe some cars. A Dodge, a Mercury. Maybe a tree. An ash tree. Nothing worth noting. He turned back to his father, who was still staring.

"I'm going to have to be going," Ray said. He waited. "I've got to get back."

He wanted to say something more. Something that might get through. "The salmon are really biting," he said. "When you get out, we'll have to do a little fishing." Another lie, of course. And even though it got no response, it was the kind of thing that might have made his father smile if it had reached him inside his haze. And that was enough. It was better than nothing.

Compassion

July 24, 1972

Dear Tricia,

I know that sometimes people in the press ask you what it's like to be the President's daughter. You might want to tell them some of the unique details that only you know about me. For instance, tell them how I'm the life of the party at Christmas, always playing piano so everyone can sing along. And make sure you tell them that I don't use sheet music. Tell them I have all the melodies stored in my head. You might also want to tell about how I often make phone calls before dinner. I call people who might be sick or mourning or having hard luck. Even though no one knows about these calls I make, they are important to me because I know from experience that you receive very few calls when you're down on your luck. A President has a responsibility to remember such people in their time of need.

You might want to tell the story of how I called Teddy Kennedy's son up the night before his amputation. Nobody's family deserves to endure such a tragedy, not even the Kennedys. So despite the fact that Big Teddy is always trying to crucify me, I called little Teddy up to give him some words of encouragement.

And trust me, a pep talk from the President can go a long way, but not all Presidents make time for this kind of contact. The public should know of the things their President is doing after hours, behind closed doors. I don't remember what little Teddy said to me. He was kind of doped up for his operation, but I'm sure he was grateful. Who wouldn't be? This is the kind of thing people should know about your father. Feel free to use this anecdote if you're ever asked what the President does when he's not running the country.

Love, Daddy

La Casa Pacifica

When they got back to San Clemente that first day—after the resignation—Pat and Dick didn't talk. They just went to their separate rooms and retired. Dick collapsed in his bed and slept straight through the evening and night. And when he woke at dawn the following morning, his first day as the only resigned president of the United States, he rubbed his eyes, farted, and rolled over in bed trying to get his bearings.

He was in California, that much he knew. There's a smell in the air in California that is unmistakable to him. It's the ocean and the warm earth and the sweat of his father and the phlegm of his brother and tomato gravy on toast and oatmeal and lemonade and the sweet talcum his mother wore. It all comes flooding back whenever he crosses the state line, but now even though he knew he was in his home state, something seemed wrong. Something seemed so Washington about his surroundings.

His gold-plated pen set stood at attention on his desk, waiting for him. It was the one Ike had given him, the one that should have been packed away in a box somewhere in a Mack truck traveling the flat highways of Kansas on its way home from the White House. And framed Duke diploma on the wall above his dresser, another White House item. And his autographed Tommy John baseball sat on the dresser. And there was more—his dictation machine, his tie rack, his first-edition copy of *The Grapes of Wrath*,

the Milhous family Bible. All of this stuff was supposed to be crated
up and en route to California via Mayflower Movers. But here it
was, glaring at him, denying him his accurate reference points.

There was only one explanation. Pat must have packed the
items separately and carried them in her suitcases, thinking he
would need to wake surrounded by the things that would remind
him of who he was. Then in the night while he slept, she must
have infiltrated his bedroom and scattered the artifacts about in an
effort to make it look and feel as if they hadn't moved cross-
country after all.

He shuffled across the room and picked up the baseball. Then
he took it back to bed with him. Under the covers, he fingered
the seams, gripped the ball as Tommy John might have—fastball,
curve, slider. He imagined himself on the mound, taking the sign
from his catcher, shaking the sign off, then stretching. With a peek
over his shoulder toward the runner on first, he quickly stepped
off the rubber, wheeled, and fired the ball to his first baseman,
successfully picking off a potential base stealer and ending the inning.

Who was this wife of his who had done this thing for him—
secretly unpacking her husband's things in the night and setting
them out on display for him? Not only had Pat stuck with him all
these years, but now when her own life had been reduced to this
puddle of seclusion behind the brick walls of La Casa Pacifica, she
had done this thing, this small but beautiful gesture of foolish,
undying sympathy. Maybe he would thank her if he could find
any humble words left in himself. But for the time being he chose
to just stay there in the bed, huddled under his covers with his
autographed baseball and all those other presidential reminders
hovering around him, whispering, "Good morning, Mr. President."

Phlebitis

When it flared up like this, Dick could convince himself that the phlebitis was the only thing wrong in his life. In that way it was a blessing.

The clot had settled down in his left calf but there was no telling how long its nap would be. Any minute the thing could have started its very short journey to his tired heart. Dr. Wiley had said, "If you look at this clot cross-eyed, it'll kill you." And the anticoagulants weren't working. But Dick was in no hurry to set the surgery date. A leg the size of a baby whale, and the pain that went with it, kept him focused, kept his mind off his other miseries. And anyway, there was a country to run. Ford was clearly hopeless and certainly the Congress hadn't allocated a two-hundred-thousand-dollar budget and given the resigned president a staff of twenty assistants so he could go fishing. Everyone knew Nixon would go on running the nation even though he had resigned. The only difference was, now he was expected to do it from the Western White House. So there was no time for self-pity or medical procedures.

In the morning, he rose and squeezed that swollen throbbing leg of his into a pair of suit pants. Then the shirt, tie, jacket, and so forth. The suit was navy wool pinstripe, the shirt a pale presidential blue perma-press, and pure power-yellow silk wrapped itself in a tight Windsor knot around his gobbler neck. He thought the limp in his walk gave him dignity as he stepped into the dining room for his morning round of meetings.

They were all there with coffee and clipboards at the ready— the assistants, the aides, the secretaries—the whole transition team. The California Cabinet, as Dick called them. They rose when Dick entered and they said in unison, "Good morning, Mr. President." He nodded, took his seat at the head of the table, and motioned for them to be seated as well.

Of course Dick noticed the odd way they all seemed to be wringing their hands that morning. Probably just worried about my phlebitis, he told himself. He began, "Good morning, everyone. All right, let's get to it. I have two items on my agenda this morning. Let's start with the election. Miller, I want you to give me an update on whether or not Ford's people have contacted my people in Texas yet. These are valuable contacts, and I don't want Ford to blow it with them. We're going to need their continued support. Put some pressure on Rockefeller's people too if you have to. He'll get after Ford."

Miller said nothing, just nodded, sucked in his lower lip, and pretended to be scribbling something on his pad. Dick said, "You all right, Miller? You look like you're the one with a clot on its way to his ticker instead of me. Did you get my Ford campaign memo or not?"

"Yes, sir. I got it, Mr. President," Miller said.

"Well all right then. Get on it."

"Yes, sir."

"Now, the next item on the agenda is a sticky one, and I suspect it will take the better part of the morning." Dick waited for a reaction but saw nothing in their faces. None of them looked at him directly. Their eyes seemed to have retreated into their skulls like bears hiding in caves, waiting to pounce.

Dick looked back at his notes. Then he said, "Gentlemen . . ." The clot in his leg yawned and sent a red-hot chill up the inside of his thigh. He winced and went on. "All right," he said, "this is the sixty-four-thousand-dollar question. Are you ready?" Still none of them made eye contact. Dick ignored it. They were a moody bunch, this California Cabinet. "The question is this," said Dick. "Here it is. I want to know what in the hell we are going to do about the economy once Ford gets himself reelected?"

No one moved at first. Then the bears stirred in their caves. The former president said, "Well, I'm waiting." Nothing. "Haven't any of you begun a battle plan on this? I sent the economy memo out weeks ago." Still nothing. Then finally, Papa Bear spoke. It was Powers—Galvin Edward Powers—head secretary of the Administrative Transition Team.

Powers cleared his throat so hard he nearly brought something up the way Harold used to when he wanted sympathy. "Mr. President," Powers said.

"What the hell is it?" demanded Dick. "What's this about, Powers? Speak up."

"Mr. President, today is the twenty-eighth."

"God damn it, Powers. I know what the fucking date is. What's your point?"

"Sir, it's the twenty-eighth of February."

"Are you trying to be a comedian, Powers? Is this a joke of some sort? Have I forgotten your wedding anniversary or something?"

"Mr. President. Sir, there isn't going to be any economic recovery plan coming out of the Western White House."

"Why the hell not, you buffoon?"

"Because our work is done here, sir."

"What do you mean our work is done? Ford's got an election to win. We've got a country to run."

"Mr. President, the transition team was only hired to work here at San Clemente for six months. Congress only allotted enough money to pay our salaries through February. They're sending us back today, sir. You've known that since last August when we arrived." Powers tried to look sheepish, but Dick could see the vindictive grin of Harold lurking behind Powers's false eyes.

"This is absurd," Dick said. "Do you think Jerry Ford knows his ass from his elbow? Do you think just because he doesn't take my phone calls that he's actually running this country? Do you think just because my leg looks like a giant Fig Newton that I am incapable of seeing this thing through?"

"Sir, I don't know about any of that. But our work is done and we're going back to Washington today. And the doctors say if you don't have that leg of yours operated on, you're going to die. Do you understand that? This isn't a football game, sir. We can't go into sudden-death overtime and just keep on playing until somebody scores. It's over."

Now all the bastards were looking at him. Now they had the courage to poke their dumb faces out of their safe caverns. Like grieving parents, these bears looked at him, like forlorn, dour-faced Quaker bears. He would have liked to have blowtorched the whole lot of them and watched their fur catch, and giggled at them as they rolled around on the floor howling in agony, the flames licking up the polyester carpeting and engulfing the window curtains until the whole place went up in a gallant blaze.

The fire in his thigh raged. But he managed to stand, smile, and nod at his inquisitors. "Fuck you," he said. "Fuck you all to hell. You think I need you? You're a bunch of pansy-ass losers, and I hope your careers are ruined. I hope they discover oil under the fields you couldn't drill while you were here trying to leech off of me. If any of you ever tries to make anything respectable of yourselves, I'll call every news agency in D.C. and I'll make damn sure they know you all volunteered to work for Tricky Dick when he was at his trickiest. How do you like that, you fuckers?"

None of the men around the dining-room table said a word. They hung their heads, every last one of them. Silenced. And so Dick Nixon straightened himself up, grabbed his clipboard, and limped out of the room in triumph.

Dick got as far as his bedroom door, and then he collapsed in a heaving heap of hot pain. His eyes rolled back in his head and instantly he was aware of his blood pressure dropping. Blood began seeping into his abdominal cavity. On the floor, writhing, Nixon called out to his valet, "Manolo. Is that you, Manolo? I'm not going to get out of here alive, Manolo. Go get Pat. Hurry."

. . .

Two days later, Dick woke up with tubes up his nose, a catheter in his cock, and an IV needle in his arm. Sitting in the corner, obviously unaware that her husband was waking up finally, Pat Nixon bit into a Quarter Pounder with cheese and chuckled at something *Bonanza*'s Little Joe said on the TV. "Got one of them hamburgers for me?" Dick asked.

Later, after Pat had spoon-fed Dick some ice shavings and given him her Hallmark card pep talk ("You've just got to be strong, blah, blah, blah"), Dick napped some more. When he woke up again, there was big dumb Jerry Ford's gray face staring at him from the doorway, going, "Oh my God. My God, Mr. President."

Nixon said, "Relax, Jerry, I'm not dead yet." Then he cranked his electric bed up and said, "Now listen, Jerry, I want to know if you've contacted my people in Texas yet."

Clippings

Ray's hair was never much to look at. It was always a bit kinky and fried out on the ends, and he went gray far too early. And lately, what with the treatments and everything else, it's been thinning uncontrollably. Ray finds hunks of it on his pillow in the morning, and recently he noticed Beth bought one of those hair traps for the shower drain. Still, it was the only hair Ray had and he wanted it to last him to the end.

So for a few months now, he's been letting the ragged remains of his frizzy gray hair grow. It's uneven and patchy, and he has no intention of seeing a barber anytime soon either. But when Beth says she's going to give his shaggy gray hair a trim, he obliges—doesn't even put up a fight. What's the worst that could happen? It's just hair.

He peels off his sweater and button-collar oxford. He gets a towel to wrap around his neck. He lays newspaper on the floor. He sets his desk chair atop the papers in the center of the room, sits in the chair wrapped up in an old beach towel, waiting for her to go to work.

Around him moldy old books rise up—an enormous collage of characters and events from his past, intertwined in ways he will never again be able to differentiate. One character's life bleeds into the next, reincarnations of one another, doing each other immeasurable harm as they trudge forth toward their forgettable resolutions.

Many of the books in this room remain unread. He meant to read them all at one time or another, but they just kept piling up over the years. He couldn't keep up. And when he tried to return to something he'd bought years before, he could no longer remember why he had wanted to read it in the first place.

A dull gray light filters through the curtains. Outside, a wintry storm is brewing—not a blizzard exactly, just a steady, heavy, big-flaked snowfall. Dependable. There'll be a few inches by morning and it probably won't stop there. Beth comes in with her scissors, comb, and brush in hand like a surgeon about to cut the years out of him, about to give him renewed life—a quadruple bypass, a skin graft, the removal of a malignant lump.

She moves in with the comb first, circling him in the chair. She combs the hair straight down over his forehead and ears. She's delicate in the thin spots, as if his scalp is somehow more sensitive there, as if the hair in those spots might last longer if she's not too rough with it. His skin tingles from the top of his head right down to his toes as she runs the comb through. He shuts his eyes and lets the electricity search for a resting place.

They're not together like this much these days, what with the chores, engagements, trips to the doctor, various affairs of the home—living at its mundane best. Good days bring small pleasures like a game of backgammon, a fireside chat, a haircut.

The room is quiet as snow. Beth circles his chair, combing and snipping, more tentative than a real barber. He says nothing, stares straight ahead out the window as she moves quietly around him. The daylight, what's left of it, begins to fade.

She trims the hairs along his neck. At his feet, the newspaper is open to the editorial section. There's a cartoon titled "Nixon in Hell," as if the misguided slob didn't suffer enough hell already. Ray remembers watching Nixon resign. He remembers wondering how Nixon held back the tears. Ray imagines when Nixon buries his wife, there will be a picture of him in the paper, his whole face flooded with tears. There will be no stopping it then. Ray wonders if Pat was Nixon's first love or if there had been others before her.

Steely scissors in hand, Beth says, "It's getting dark already. It gets dark so early now. I can't get used to it."

After a while more she says, "Okay, done."

Ray rises slowly so as not to disturb the loose hairs everywhere. He goes to look in the mirror. His hair looks lousy, but it's no fault of Beth's. She did the best she could with what she had to work with. She's cleaned up his neckline, and the wisps over his ears have retreated and fallen in line, curving in a solid wide white-wall. He feels lighter, younger, even though the bald spots are more noticeable now.

Ray smiles at Beth. She licks her fingertips and mats down a cowlick on the top of Ray's head. Then she kisses him, pats his ass, and winks at him as if to say, "Got any plans tonight, Big Boy?"

Later, after he's gathered the newspapers and slid the chair back under the desk, he shakes the gray hairs out of the towel and then sweeps them into a neat pile. Outside the snow swirls. He remembers when he was a boy how he hated the barbershop because he couldn't keep his hair clippings from landing on the lollipop the barber gave him. What good was a free lollipop if it was covered in hair?

Ray wisks the pile of hair into a dust pan and dumps it on top of the newspapers. For a moment, he contemplates the fate of Richard Nixon's soul again. Then he crumples the pile of papers with the hair wrapped neatly inside.

He decides he'll throw this ball of hair and newspaper into the trash, and then he and Beth might play some backgammon or read together beside the fireplace. Over the pages of some book of poems, Beth will wink at him again. And he will wink back at this woman who has saved his life more than once.

Ray runs a hand through his hair like he's seen movie stars do. Suddenly he understands that it's a good thing that he's going to beat Beth to the grave. In fact, it's pure luck. After all, what would he do without her. He simply wouldn't know *what* to do. Even hell would be better.

Ray's shoulders and back itch. But he doesn't fuss about it. Instead, he just slips back into his shirt and decides it's time to make an honest woman of Beth. Just like that. Tonight, sporting his fresh haircut he will get down on one knee like a schoolboy and ask Beth to marry his sorry ass. And next week, if his luck holds out, they'll pack up the car and drive to Vegas. They'll find themselves a neon chapel and tie the knot before a neon reverend and a neon Jesus. They'll tie the knot before they run out of time. Before Ray is completely bald. Before it's too late.

These Days

When it gets like this, Dick wishes he could crawl under a rock. If somebody would have assassinated him before the Watergate shit hit the fan, he'd be a hero by now. But that would require being dead, of course, and he's not sure he can trust the living; even Kennedy's secrets are out now (not that the bastard didn't deserve it). Dick wishes he were a turtle. He'd suck his legs and oblong head into his shell and never come out.

Pat would be the only one to miss him. And if she were smart, she'd get over it soon enough. These days, now that the California Cabinet has returned to D.C., Pat is Dick's sole contact with the rest of humanity. Dick is infinitely grateful that he did not marry Vera Louise, not that she would have had him anyway. She saw way back then that he'd end up a complete failure, a disgrace even to this hideous species that daily paves the way to its own dinosaurian end.

Only the turtles will survive. And the cockroaches, of course. It's those hard shells they wear. You're safe when you have a place to hide. If you stripped a turtle of its shell, it would die instantly of humiliation.

These days, when he's alone in his library, sweating in his leather wing back, he just stares. A mountain of legal books stares back. An infinite number of hiding places in those books, but he doesn't even have the energy to open one and begin the battle.

Maybe he deserves this misery. He gave the bastards the sword, and they twisted it with relish, and if he were in their shoes, he would have done the same damn thing. It's a Bay of Pigs out there beyond the walls of this estate. A bay of his own making.

Pat knocks on the door and enters. Sometimes she just sits with him in silence. Sometimes she fixes him a drink. Sometimes she reads the paper to him. As if he'd want to know what's going on out there. He hasn't spoken in weeks except to whimper a thank-you to her. If she were not here, he imagines he'd be in a straitjacket some place.

Pat says, "You won't find forgiveness in this room." She says, "You won't find salvation in the spines of these law books." And, "The man I married doesn't sit on his backside just because he got clubbed over the head with a baseball bat."

He doesn't even look up at her. He is a corpse. A soggy green lump of flesh waiting to stiffen. There are certain luxuries to catatonia. The people around you don't expect much from you once they observe that you're not even capable of blinking your own eyes without assistance. Sitting there, paralyzed like this, the only sound he ever hears is Pat's voice. She loves him. The stupid stupid woman.

One day, she came in wearing only her satin pink robe. She hoisted her old varicose thigh up on the armchair of his recliner and flashed him her beaver. He blinked. Involuntarily. They fucked like teenagers exploring each other for the first time. He could hear the beach applauding its approval in the distance as she mounted him. He pinched her dry nipples and she giggled. Then he cried.

Afterward, lying like tarnished spoons on the den floor, he began drifting back into himself. This time though, he fought it, reaching his hand around Pat's hip to the skin of her once-taut belly. Running his fingers over Pat's stretch marks, Dick imagined Pat dead, reduced to a settling pile of dust, periodically stirred by the aimless, sweeping bristles of Dick's memory.

When Pat had had enough of Dick's dick, he went outside and wandered the grounds. It was the first time he'd done this in ages. On a walkway near the front gate, he saw an ant farm. He wished he had a can of Raid. The worker ants scurried about mindlessly, sacrificing themselves for the good of the colony, rushing this way and that, risking their futile lives to retrieve sap globules or hunks of sand for their fellow ants. Dick swiped his big old size thirteen shoe across the top of the anthill, sending the little buggers into furious spasms. For a while Dick watched them fall in and begin the rebuilding process. He contemplated getting some Raid and finishing them off, putting them out of their misery, but on second thought decided to just pick up one unlucky worker by one of its legs and carry it up to his porch steps, where he dropped the silly little creature into a spiderweb and watched him get devoured.

"You won't find redemption in those law books," Pat had said, but she was wrong. Salvation does lie in the law. If not there, then where? He decides that one day very soon, he will contact his lawyers and they will begin the battle. They will tie those fucking tapes up in so many suits and countersuits that no one will ever know the real Dick Nixon. There will be nothing left to kick around. Just a vague memory of the Open Door policy and a few other miscellaneous foreign policy achievements. Long after his death, the lawyers and biographers and poets and moviemakers will still be fighting it out, trying to get at the essence of Dick Nixon. But it will all be conjecture, educated guesses, fiction. He'll be deep in his shell, free at last. And safe. Finally.

Diddling

I wanted to go bowling. Or miniature golfing. Or go-carting. Something fun. Something silly. But you don't exactly just wander into a bowling alley with Richard Nixon and ask for a lane. Ray could have gone—nobody ever recognizes poets. And I certainly have no fear of the public eye. But Dick wasn't ready to roll a gutter ball in front of a nosy bowling-alley crowd.

"Besides," Dick said, "I'm a lousy bowler. You two would kick my ass." He said to Ray, "I bet you're one of them damn finesse bowlers."

"Just like Fred Flintstone," Ray said. "I'm a ballerina in a bowling alley."

"Don't they have a bowling alley in the basement of the White House?" I asked.

"As a matter of fact, they do," said Dick.

"You know what you ought to do," said Ray. "You ought to call up the White House and tell them you're bringing a couple of friends over to bowl a few lines. Tell him to keep a lane free for us, and we'll fly out to Washington and make a weekend of it."

"Yeah," I said. "Reagan owes you that much."

"Very funny, smart-ass," Dick said, smacking me on the back of the head. He liked to do this. It was usually just an affectionate little smack.

Ray laughed and said, "The kid's right. Call old Ronnie up. Tell him your friends voted for Carter. Maybe that will get a rise out of him and he'll want to challenge us to a game or two."

"You fuckers didn't really vote for that putz, did you?" Dick asked. Then, before we could answer, he said, "Never mind, I don't want to know."

I said, "I was too young to vote in that election, Dick. I think I was only like eleven or twelve at the time. But we had a mock election in my grammar school, and your man kicked Jimmy's ass."

"Smart kids," Dick said.

Ray went, "Yeah, too bad the country's not run by ten-year-olds."

Dick's retort: "He said they were eleven and twelve, so go screw yourself, poet." Then Dick said, "I got an idea, why don't you bastards give me a hand cleaning out my garage."

Ray said he'd be up for helping with the garage.

"You got to be kidding," I said. "I didn't come all this way to clean your fucking garage."

But I could see I was fighting a losing battle. It was late autumn. In California the trees never lose their leaves, but there's something about the air that's different in the fall. It turns on you around the time that tree branches in the real world are busy baring themselves to the coming winter. And trust me, it's hard enough to get a dying poet and a resigned president to whoop it up in the summer, but trying to do it on a damp gray November afternoon is just plain foolish. So I conceded. Dick ordered a pizza and we cleaned the garage.

Ray's one of these guys who focuses on one thing for a long time until he gets it perfect. Slow and methodical. He spent nearly the whole day cleaning the muddy tips of Dick's gardening tools. He polished those damn things till he could see himself in them. Once in a while he'd get sidetracked by something. Like he'd see a horsehair paintbrush and he'd break into some story about how his old man taught him to paint. There'd be no real point to the story. The punch line would be something like, "I tried to paint the whole damn ceiling with a paintbrush, and my old man comes in and says, 'No, you idiot, they got rollers for that.' " At the end of each story, Dick would pretend to be amused; then he'd tell Ray to get back to work.

"Sometimes I think maybe I'm wasting my time with you," Dick told Ray at one point.

"Maybe you are," Ray said.

I said, "Sometimes I think maybe I'm wasting my time with both of you."

"Maybe you are," Ray said again.

One of the stories Ray told was about a girl he knew in graduate school, some woman he had an affair with while Peggy was raising their two kids. "I once knew a girl," Ray said, pulling on his cigarette and polishing a set of shrub shears, "who required at least forty-five minutes of clitoral diddling before she'd come. Now that was a waste of time."

"Jesus," said Dick. "Forty-five minutes. Jesus."

"At least."

"Did she go crazy when it finally happened?" I asked, sitting down on the garage floor and pretending to sort through a box of car supplies.

"Sure. She went crazy," Ray said.

"Well, then why was it a waste of time?" Dick wanted to know. "I mean, what more can you ask of a woman?"

"That's one way to look at it," said Ray.

I wanted to do my part to propel the conversation forward, so I said, "There's nothing like a screeching woman wrapping her legs around you and begging for more, eh?"

"Like you would know," Dick said.

"Nothing like it, indeed," Ray told me. "But still, forty-five minutes is forty-five minutes. On a good day, I could write a couple of poems in forty-five minutes. You've only got so many minutes allotted to you in this life, and orgasms are invisible. Poems last." Ray dragged hard on his cigarette and reached for a dust rag.

I asked them, "Ever feel like your whole life is one big clitoral diddle?"

"Never," said Ray.

"Never," said Dick.

"Oh come on."

Dick said, "I was the fucking president, you numb nuts, pimple-faced putz! You going to call that a clitoral diddle?"

"Sounds like a diddle to me," said Ray.

"Listen, you fucker, you sit around drinking your vanilla mist coffee and sucking on cigarettes, writing your worthless piddle all day long. You think anybody reads the shit? If you think anybody cares but you and all your other asinine writer friends, you're a fool. You're the diddle! Both of you are diddles."

"My life isn't a complete waste, Dick," I said. "After all, here I am serving the needs of two of the free world's most important men."

Dick flipped me the bird and went on cleaning. He cleans a garage the same way he does everything else. Runs from one job to the next. One minute he's vacuuming cobwebs out of a corner. Then he sees some nails sticking out of a wall, so he shuts off the vacuum, grabs a pliers, and starts bending and twisting and yanking at the nails. "Somebody might hurt themselves," he said as he yanked on a particularly stubborn and rusty one. Meanwhile, the cobwebs he was working on gently fluttered in the corners as he stirred up a breeze with all his huffing and puffing over the nails. And then the next thing I knew, he had abandoned the nails and started running around the garage chasing a sluggish autumn fly. It was comical, it really was.

I was just standing out of their way, pretending to be sweeping. I made one little pile of dust. Then I sneezed and sat down on the garage floor again to nurse my allergies. Dick hollered at me, "Come on, you lazy ass." But he could see he wasn't going to get much work out of me, so he said, "Why don't you go down to the security gate and see if our pizza is here yet."

I said, "Why can't they bring it up to the house for us? For that matter, don't you have servants who can clean this stupid garage for you?"

I knew the answer to that. By definition, servants are people who do other people's work. "I'll do my own work, and I'll do it my way," Dick said.

"Then why do you have us helping you?" I asked.

"Shut up and go get the pizza," Dick said.

So I gave in and walked out the side door, but I didn't want to miss anything, so I stood out there for a while and eavesdropped. They started talking about the value of diddling again. Ray was saying, "Fine, but afterward, what's left?"

"That lingering womanly perfume on your fingertips, for one thing," Dick said. "That smell is a reminder."

"But sooner or later you've got to wash your hands, and then what have you got?"

"You call yourself a poet? I thought you sons of bitches were supposed to be romantic."

"What's romantic about smelling like a vagina?"

"Everything, you yoddle. Don't you see the power? It lingers. You can't even wash it off that easy. It puts up a fight. Clings to you. Like it's grateful or something."

"What about the next day? When it's all gone."

"The next day she looks at you across a steaming meatloaf on the dinner table and her eyes sparkle or something, and you know what she's thinking about? She's remembering what you did to her the night before. And maybe while you're out the day after that, and she's doing the laundry, she starts thinking about it, and she gets all hot, and then she squats down in a pile of your dirty socks and boxer shorts and diddles herself! Now, are you going to tell me that forty-five-minute diddle you performed was a total waste? Look what you got her doing to herself in honor of your memory!"

"I still say a diddle is just a diddle."

"Yeah? Well, you know what I think? I think your poems are diddles. Only they're self-inflicted diddles. You're just like a lonely wife kneeling in a laundry pile. What good is that? You ever try to masturbate while fantasizing about masturbating?"

"Of course not."

"I rest my case. You're just diddling yourself when you could be diddling somebody else. I'm telling you, this is the most important lesson I ever learned in life: The only great diddle is the one you do to somebody else."

Rays asked, "Is that why you went into politics?"

"You better believe it," Dick said.

Outside the garage door, I stifled a laugh and then I figured I better get down to the gate to get that pizza before it got cold. It was a long walk down to the security entrance. I could have taken a golf cart, but I didn't feel like it. The ocean slapped at the shore behind me as I made my way down the cobblestone path to the front gate. The garden was kind of a mess at Nixon's place. I'm told it was kept up much better at one time. Same with the golf course. Nobody used it anymore so the greens were all grown over. Beautiful piece of property, but you could tell it was owned by a man who had turned out to be a failure.

By comparison, Ray's place up in Port Angeles, was tiny. And it was a total mess. At least Nixon kept up the inside of his place. Carver and his old lady were slobs. The place was cluttered with so many books and stacks of papers, you couldn't even get comfortable there. And it stunk of cigarettes. But the place was alive. It was like all that crap lying around kept him going, gave him an unstoppable momentum. He'd set down one piece of paper and then pick up another. Funny that he was the one among us who was getting ready to die. You'd never have guessed it to look at him or his place.

Maybe that was why I didn't want to clean Dick's garage. I mean, I'm not generally a lazy person. But for some reason I just couldn't bring myself to help him tidy the place up. If anything, we should have been messing it up more.

After I got the pizza from one of those Secret Service bastards who had swept the box with a metal detector and tested a piece for poison, I began the long trek back to the garage. That's when

I came up with my idea. I decided that after we ate the pizza, I'd start cleaning with gusto. I'd whirl around that garage like a cleaning tornado. Where Ray was too focused, I'd be all-encompassing. Where Dick was too scatterbrained, I'd be the finish man. We'd be the perfect team. And once the whole place was spotless, and we were standing there shaking each other's hands and patting each other on the back, I'd step back and I'd say, "You know, there's one thing that would make this garage look better."

They'd both look at me quizzically and say, "What's that?"

And I'd say, "This . . ." Then I'd grab a rake or a broom or a baseball bat and I'd run around that garage like a raving lunatic having a manic fit. I'd diddle that garage for all it was worth. I'd knock down everything we'd stacked, smash every squeegeed window, overturn every box we'd packed, bash every breakable object in sight, and empty all the garbage cans of their dust and other crap. Then in a sneezing rage, I'd say, "There, that's better."

And maybe Dick wouldn't appreciate it at first, but sooner or later he'd see what I'd done for him, and he'd thank me. It might not happen right away. It could take years. But someday he'd see what I'd done and why I'd done it, and he'd thank me. Either that, or he'd kill me. But I was willing to take that chance.

I'd like to be able to say that I carried out my plan, but the truth is, when I got back to the garage, we ate the pizza and finished cleaning, but in the end I couldn't bring myself to mess the place up. We had worked so hard. And everything was in its place just like Dick liked it. Maybe I wimped out. Maybe I did the wrong thing. But I just couldn't mess it up.

On the way out of the garage, Dick took one last look around, smiled, gave me and Ray the thumbs-up, and then shut out the light. That was the last time all three of us were ever together in one place.

747

Real men fly their own airplanes. But that was yet another thing Dick never learned to do. Even when Harold was flying crop dusters against the doctor's orders and had offered to let Dick take the stick, Dick had declined, afraid Harold might suck up too much pesticide and croak right there in the cockpit, and then what? How would poor little Dick Nixon find his way back to earth without Harold?

So if you're too afraid to learn, you let somebody else do the flying. Nixon logged more hours on *Air Force One* than any other president. That said something. And now he was logging more hours on American Airlines than any resigned president. That wasn't saying much.

It's amazing who you can bump into on an airplane. People you knew in past lives, people you know now, people you wish you never knew. Probably when he got home later today and told Pat who he saw sitting back in coach, she wouldn't even believe it. Who would?

It couldn't hurt to invite the poor slob up to first class, he figured. After all, except for a few omnipresent Secret Service guys, he damn near had all of first class to himself. And he already had a couple of drinks in him, so what the hell. So that's just what he did; he grabbed the arm of a passing stewardess and said, "See that sorry-looking bastard back in coach? The bald guy with the

big dumb harmless-looking smile on his face? He's right there,"
he said, pointing. "About halfway back on the left. By the emer-
gency exit door."

The stewardess reclaimed her forearm from Nixon's sweaty
palm, squinted, saw which man he meant, and nodded.

"You know who that is?" he asked the stewardess, who
showed no sign of recognition. "That's George McGovern,
sweety. Once a candidate for the Oval Office, but you're probably
too young to remember him. I want you to bring him a drink on
me, and then I want you to tell him I got an empty seat right next
to me, bought and paid for, and I want to offer it to him. Tell
him the president of the United States of America requests his
presence up in first class."

The stewardess snarled, "You mean ex-president, don't you?"

Nixon said, "Don't get sassy, sweety. It doesn't become you."
Then he said as she walked away, "And hey, get me another scotch
while you're at it, will you, honey?"

Nixon was slurping his Chivas when McGovern fell into the seat
beside him. Staring straight ahead at the seat back in front of him,
McGovern nodded and said, "Thanks for the drink, Dick."

Nixon said, "No sense wasting a perfectly good first-class
seat."

"Mighty neighborly of you," McGovern said, and Dick
couldn't tell for sure if maybe there was a hint of sarcasm in Mc-
Govern's voice or not. Perhaps he only imagined it.

The men didn't shake hands or even raise their plastic glasses
to one another. There was a long moment of silence. McGovern
appeared to be eyeing a Secret Service man two rows over.

Nixon turned on his air vent and reading lamp. It was something to do with his hands. Then he offered this: "I'm coming
back from a fishing trip. I was up in the Pacific Northwest fishing.
With a couple of writers actually, if you can believe it. Can you
imagine me fishing with a poet?"

McGovern didn't respond. Stone-faced.

Nixon said, "I suppose it wouldn't be much of a shock if a guy like you went fishing with a poet. But a guy like me is supposed to play golf with bank presidents and stockbrokers. You know what I mean?"

McGovern offered a halfhearted smirk and a nod, still eyeing that Secret Service man.

"I mean, you Democrats read a lot of that sort of shit, don't you? Poetry, I mean. That's your thing, right?" Dick said, trying to get a rise.

McGovern smiled more earnestly now. "Some of us read it," he said. "Some of us play golf with bank presidents."

"The first time I remember reading a poem I actually liked," Nixon said, "I was sitting on the toilet in the White House. Good place to read a poem, don't you think? On the toilet, I mean, not the White House. Anyway, some aide or somebody had left this book of poems on the tank alongside my *Reader's Digest* and *TV Guide*. And I remember picking the damn thing up by mistake and reading this one poem called 'Looking for Work.' This was at the time of the whole you-know-what-gate fiasco, and I knew *I'd* be out looking for work soon enough. Anyway the poem is about this guy who dreams about eating trout for breakfast, and then his wife wakes him up, and he feels the house tilt as he's trying to get up out of bed, and then the poem just ends real suddenly with the line 'My new shoes wait gleaming by the door.' I remember I didn't know what the fuck it meant, but somehow it spoke to me and to what I was going through, you know?"

McGovern was still as stone. "I think I know what you mean," he said.

Was he being snide? No way to tell. So Nixon said, "Anyway, it was the only clean shit I took that whole year I think. Lot of constipation that year as you can imagine. Haven't been the same since." Then he fidgeted with his air blower again and called the stewardess over and ordered another round. "Nice calves on that little honey," he said, pointing at the stewardess. "I like a good strong calf muscle on a woman, don't you, George?"

McGovern sipped what remained of his highball and said, "It

depends." Then he polished off the last few drops of his drink.

Nixon elbowed him and said, "That's it. Drink up, my friend."

A slurping moment passed between them in the tinkle-jaggle of melting ice cubes in plastic cups. Nixon wiped his brow with his American Airlines cocktail napkin. The reading light bounced off his bald spot and scattered sweaty light between them. "What the fuck was I just talking about?" he said.

"Poetry," said McGovern in what might have been a pseudo-sensitive tone, as if to mock.

"Oh yeah. Whatever. How about you, George? Where are you coming from?"

McGovern had been visiting his daughter in Seattle. That's all he offered. Then he rested his head on the top back of his seat, stared straight ahead at the seat in front of him, reclined a bit, stared some more.

Nixon sucked down his fresh scotch and said, out of nowhere, "This friend of mine. The poet. He's got cancer eating its way up to his brain."

"I'm sorry to hear that," McGovern said, and Dick thought he could tell George meant it.

"Smoker," Dick said. "Started in the lungs."

"That's always the way," said George.

"Another round," Dick called to the stewardess. Then he pulled two fat Cuban cigars out of his shirt pocket and offered one to McGovern. George accepted. Nixon lit it for him and then lit his own. They puffed like smokestacks. "Kennedy smoked cigars like these," Nixon said. "They couldn't get the smell out of *Air Force One* for years. Now his descendants, *your* liberal friends in Washington, want to ban smoking on airplanes altogether," he said, pointing his cigar a McGovern as if to accuse. "You know, I was surrounded by TB my whole life and never got it. All through my childhood, I lived with lungers. Thought for sure I'd die young." He paused to puff his cigar. Then he said, "Now look at me. Here I am. Spared by the hand of God so I could fuck the Constitution up the ass."

George nodded as if to agree. Cigar smoke billowed and clouded out in front of them. First class all to themselves. The Cuban fog mimicked the scotch cloud in Nixon's head. "Cubans," Nixon said.

"Cubans," McGovern said.

Dick ordered yet another drink for himself and one for McGovern even though they still had fresh ones in front of them.

"Did I ever tell you about my brother Harold? The one with TB?" Nixon asked.

McGovern said, "No. I'd like to hear about him." Dick was sure George was being sincere. But damn, you could never tell about those Democrats. Still, why would George say he wanted to hear about Harold unless he meant it. Dick started slow, with Harold's death, and he worked backward from there. Eventually, the floodgates opened in that smoky 747. Maybe it was the scotch, maybe it was just time to wrap things up. Nixon pulled the shade down on his little airplane window and told McGovern the whole story. Everything. The TB, the cabin in Prescott, barking at the wheel of fortune, bedpans, oil wells under the grocery store, the swamp out back, Sunday school lessons, Arthur's deathbed breakfast of tomato gravy on toast, the buggy incident, the bluebird fantasies, Vera Louise, the dry lemon groves, Glenda Newcomb's crotch, the railroad tracks, all of it. All nine lives. In no particular order. He even made mention of his John Deere tractor.

McGovern nodded, looked concerned at the right moments, frowned vaguely when Nixon wanted him to. And Nixon, he was teetering beyond the edge of sloppy drunk now. He spilled it all—a lifetime of fear and failure. The lifetime of a Nixon. No more shell games, every secret exposed.

Eventually, Dick even got to the part about Jessie Lynch and Larry Easton and Harold's expertise with electricity. He was giving McGovern everything he had to offer. "This is it," he said. "This is the whole story. This is the eighteen and half minutes of missing tape. But it isn't about the Nixon presidency. And it isn't about how the Cubans killed Kennedy. And it isn't about how CREEP sabotaged Teddy's fucking car at Chappaquiddick. And it's not the Bay of Pigs. And it's not Woodward and fucking Bernstein or Robert fucking Altman, either. This is just my pathetic fucking life. Secrets of a lifetime, of several lifetimes— dominoes of failure. I'm entrusting it all to you, George. If I were you, I'd stick a butcher knife in it and twist it around a few times. With relish. But I'm banking on the fact that you're not me."

Dick wiped the sweat from his forehead, finished off his drink, and then sort of half smiled ironically, like a man who had just made his last move in a long and tedious game of chess, as if the word "checkmate" had finally just issued from his lipless mouth.

"You see, George, I'm a more glorious fuckup than ever walked the face of our sad old planet. Except maybe for Hitler," he said after a short silence. "I cast a shadow everywhere I go. It wasn't my intention. It just happened. This old airliner is eclipsing Mother Earth right now, as a matter of fact. And all we're doing is having a drink together. Bygones—trying to make sense of things."

Dick turned to George, and for the first time in all the years they'd known each other, they looked directly into one another's eyes. Nixon held McGovern's gaze for a long moment, and then finally he said, "I'm going to die soon, George."

George raised his eyebrows in protest or perhaps just drunken confusion.

"No, no, don't try to tell me it's not true," Nixon said. "I know my time is almost up. And don't start feeling sorry for me. You're going to die soon too, you know." Dick laughed and elbowed his companion. "I think I want a closed casket," Dick said, serious now, "no lying in state or any of that nonsense, and no burial in Washington either—I won't give those bastards another chance to crucify me. God, I hope somebody makes sure they give me a good shave. You know how thick my damn beard gets. Did you know that hair and fingernails keep growing after you're dead?"

George nodded. Then he hiccupped.

"George, you would have made a lousy president, just like that Carter fuck. But you're a decent man. I just want to tell you that. I'm no one to judge, but you're good people, George. So, McGovern, old foe, old sap, old goody-goody, I'm going to leave you something in my will."

George waved his hands as if to say, No no, I don't deserve anything.

Dick said, "Relax, George. I'm not giving you a million dollars or anything. My cigar collection, George. All my big old Bay o' Pigs cigars." He blew a smoke ring in George's face. "What do you think of that?"

George looked bashfully grateful, nodded, and said he'd be honored to smoke the president's cigars.

"What I oughta do," said Dick, "is put a goddamn wiretap in my coffin and give you the listening device for it." Dick waited for a reaction. George's face was drained of color.

"Come on, George," Dick said. "Can't you imagine how much fun it would be to hear Nixon saying absolutely nothing for the first time in his life?" Dick slapped George's knee and laugh-drooled on himself. Then he said in drunken earnest, "Just think, you'd be the only man with the privilege of actually tuning in and listening to my eternal silence. Whenever you got lonely, you could turn it on, light up a cigar, and have a listen."

George shook his head.

"One thing's for sure," Dick said. "You'd always know where to find me."

With that, Dick closed his eyes and leaned his head back, and in the silence that now lingered between them, Dick gradually drifted off into a deep, inebriated slumber. George McGovern wiped the corner of his eye with a cocktail napkin and asked a passing flight attendant for some peanuts and a glass of water. Then he went back to his seat in coach and left Dick there in first class with his head tilted back, mouth open, snoring and gagging a little on the phlegm in his throat.

Stroke

Some jazzy piano thing was playing on Tricia's car radio when she drove Dick home from the hospital—something far too happy and melodic. Dick asked his daughter to turn the radio off.

The Secret Service trailed behind them in a dark blue Caprice. Back at the hospital, Pat was no doubt still sitting upright in her bed, grumbling out of the right side of her limp lips. "There's nothing wrong with me," she'd be trying to say, but of course no one would understand a word of it.

Dick slumped in the passenger seat and ran a palm over his aching forehead. Then he closed his eyes and tried to remember the magnolia blossoms in the D.C. spring. All he could see was snow. The shadowy fuzz of winter memories. That mocking piano melody from the radio stepped back into his ear again, half horror-movie theme, half New Age anthem.

"Please, Tricia. I asked you to turn it off."

Tricia touched his knee. "Daddy," she said, "it is off. I turned the radio off already."

Behind the fortress walls of San Clemente, a winding drive curved past checkpoints and guards, through gates and over small bridges. Somewhere in there beyond the golf course, now grown over and untended, La Casa Pacifica stood on the shore waiting for her master to return. Tricia steered the car along its path, nodding at the security men as she passed.

A cold breeze taunted the misting waves and a gray dusk stood motionless, threatening to last forever and never turn into night. Tricia helped her father from the car and led him into his somber mansion. The agents followed at a respectful distance, their heads cast down, their hands in their pockets.

Once inside, Tricia offered to make something to eat. "You must be hungry," she said. "Some soup," she said. "It'll warm you up."

"Leave me be, dear. I'll be fine. I just need some rest."

He could hear those damn piano keys tiptoeing back, then stepping lively, smirking and jeering at him. "Godamnedest thing," he said. Then he went off to his bedroom and left Tricia there in the foyer.

Pat was in the hospital. Dying maybe. Or maybe just turning into a vegetable. Who knew. Dick went to his room, sat on the edge of his bed, and picked up the telephone. He dialed Ray's number.

"Pat's had a stroke," Dick told his friend. "She's in ICU at Pendleton."

"I know," Ray said. "I saw it on the TV. I'm sorry."

Silence hummed on the line.

"How do you go about making a poem?" Dick asked.

"I don't know yet," Ray said. "I'm still trying to figure it out."

"When you figure it out, will you let me know?"

"I promise," Ray said. Then he said, "Tell me about it."

"I was sitting at the table eating a bowl of Frosted fucking Flakes. There was one of those floppy vinyl records on the back of the cereal box. You know, the kind you can cut out and play on the phonograph."

"Yeah, I know the kind."

"It was Tom Jones singing the Frosted Flakes theme song or some damn thing, with Tony the Tiger singing backup."

"Jesus," said Ray.

"Yeah. And I was trying to cut the fucking thing out with a

paring knife. I thought I'd listen to it for a laugh and then maybe I'd give it to one of the grandkids. My cereal was getting soggy."

"Naturally."

"And Pat's standing at the counter, trying to open a jar of grapefruit juice. She's fumbling with the bottle like mad and mumbling in this kind of slurred way. I don't pay much attention at first. I mean, she's never been much of a morning person, and she'd had a few highballs the night before. But then she turns around and looks right at me and says something I can't even make out. Her mouth looks numb and lazy. And I know right away what's happening. I know it's a stroke."

"But you didn't panic."

"No. That's the thing. In my whole stupid fucked-up life it's the first time I didn't panic. My wife could have been dying, but I didn't want to scare her, so I went right on cutting that goddamn record out of the cereal box."

"Tom Jones."

"And then I eat the soggy flakes in my bowl. All the while Pat's standing at the sink, fumbling with that juice jar, and I'm thinking any minute she's going to drop it and it's going to shatter all over the kitchen."

"But you don't let on."

"No."

"Incredible."

"So then I go upstairs and wake up Tricia, who just happened to be staying with us, and I say, 'Mommy's having a stroke. Or she had a stroke. I don't know which, but we need to call Dr. Nuescheller."

"Pat didn't want to go to the hospital, right?"

"Right. She fought us all the way. That's how she is."

"I know."

"Ray?"

"Yeah, Dick."

"There is a God, right?"

"In your case, I think there's going to have to be."

"That's what I figured." Dick sat back against the headboard on his bed, still cradling the phone. Neither man said anything for a moment.

Then Ray said, "I'll call you when I figure out this poetry business."

"I'd really appreciate that."

"Keep me posted on Pat."

"I will."

Ray said, "She's tougher than me and you put together, you know."

"I know. I know. It was the same way with my mother and dad."

"It always is."

"I guess so. Did I ever tell you about what she did the morning after the resignation?"

"You mean when she put all your stuff in your bedroom while you were sleeping?"

"Yeah. I guess I told you already," Dick said. "She saved my life you know."

Again, a pause. Then finally, Ray added this: "This is not part of your punishment."

Dick said, "It isn't?"

"This is about her, not you."

"Right. Right, I know you're right."

"Call me again," Ray said, "if you need to be reminded."

"I will," said Dick. And with that both men said good night and hung up, and Dick slid himself up to the edge of the bed and just sat there, listening to the sea and staring straight ahead at nothing all night.

Sitting there like that, Dick envisioned, up the coast, Ray and Beth lying together like spoons under a feather comforter in a big comfortable bed while the waves crashed inevitably outside their bedroom window. Sweet uninterrupted sleep. The sleep of a great snoring king and his beautiful, tired queen.

Eulogy

There comes a point in your life when you can't really remember how many funerals you've attended, how many loved ones you've "waked." It's about that time that your parents start to die off. First one, and then the other. It was Ray's father who went first.

It was a sunny afternoon in May when Ray found himself in an undertaker's office with his mother. They were there to make the arrangements. Nothing fancy. Your basic burial.

Ray and his mother waited for nearly fifteen minutes in the office. The blinds were drawn and the room smelled damp. From time to time, Ray's mother sniffed back a tear, or something like a tear. At one point Ray offered Ella his handkerchief but she waved it off.

They didn't say much to each other. What was there to say? *Did Dad leave a will?* Yes. *Was there any insurance?* Some. *Would she be all right?* Fine. *And if she needed anything?* She'd call. *Would she stay in the house?* She was thinking about moving. Too many memories.

Ray's mother pushed her white hair out of her eyes and squeezed the back of Ray's hand. She was wearing clip-on earrings of all things. And rings on nearly every finger. Fake jewels, costume stuff, no wedding band. Just a hint of mascara on the eyelashes and peach lipstick to match the painted fingernails. As if the undertaker might think less of her if she'd showed up without wearing these things. Maybe she just wanted the undertaker to take notice of her appearance and remember it for future reference.

Ella checked her watch. "What's taking him so long?" she said.

Ray saw the little white hairs that had broken through along her chin. Too many to hide. And the creases around her mouth. Too many to count. Every part of her could have passed for a corpse. Except the eyes. They were as alive as a teenager's eyes. A dusty hazel—glazed, a little puffy underneath, but very much alive. "Where is that man?" she said again.

She was referring to the undertaker, of course, but she might as well have been speaking of her husband. How many times had she asked that question when Ray was growing up. "Where do you suppose your father is?" she'd say as she dropped a boiled chicken leg onto Ray's dinner plate. And "What could have become of him?" as she served up the mashed potatoes. She always said these things as if she were surprised, as if any minute now, she hoped her husband would walk through the door with some heroic tale of how he'd been helping an elderly blind woman get to the pharmacy for her medication.

They'd eat in silence, Ray and his mother and his older brother Eddie. Or rather, the boys would eat, but Ella would sit and stir her apple sauce and stare at the back door. Ray thought she was hoping for it to creak open. But one particular summer evening as Ray forced down a mouthful of brown lettuce core, his father banged into the kitchen and let the screen door slam behind him. He had been almost two hours late. It was a Friday. Ray had been watching his mother's eyes at just the moment when his father came in. That's when he saw, for the first time that he had misinterpreted his mother's hope all along. At the sight of her husband's arrival, Ella's eyes had drained of hope. There was no relief in them, no gratitude.

Before that night, Ray had always assumed she wanted the old bastard to come home. But in fact, she had been hoping all this time that he'd never return. In fact, the creak of the door opening had made her cringe. This was the first time Ray ever thought of his mother as a person, and not just as his mother. This was also the first time he realized that he was the one who had been watching the door hopefully, waiting for the familiar creak of its hinges.

"So *there* you are," Ray's mother said as the undertaker entered the office.

The undertaker looked like an undertaker. Suit of polyester, lapel a bit too wide, pant legs a bit too short. Hair sprayed in place but somehow still looking like he'd slept on it. The undertaker took off his suit coat and hung it on a coat stand, motioning to Ray and his mother not to get up. The undertaker's vest was too tight. The buttons looked as if they might pop even though the undertaker was a thin man. The undertaker offered his hand to Ray. The hand looked clean enough, but Ray almost couldn't bring himself to shake it. He knew what went on in these places. Ray shook the undertaker's hand and introduced himself. "I was his son," Ray said. "This is my mother."

"It's nice to meet you, Mrs. Carver. I hope we can lessen the burden of your loss."

"Thank you," Ray's mother said.

The undertaker reached out for her hand and held it for a moment. Ray wanted to scream. When the undertaker, whose name was Johnson, finally sat behind his enormous, immaculate, wooden desk, he looked more like a banker than an undertaker. He brought out his catalogues and began showing Ray and his mother the "options." One casket's lining came in three different colors—all soft and soothing, Johnson the undertaker promised. Another casket was available with various pressure-seal warranties (as if anyone would ever cash in on such a warranty).

Ella made her choices, occasionally checking over her shoulder to see if Ray approved. He offered support, nothing more, nothing less. What did he care about marble and pine? What difference could it possibly make? Johnson the undertaker kept nodding and saying, "An excellent choice," as if Ella were selecting wine to go with her filet in a fine restaurant. As Ray's mother made her decisions, Johnson the undertaker hits some buttons on his adding machine and jotted notes in a log book.

Ray wondered if the undertaker liked his job. Did he think of it as an art form? Was he proud of his accomplishments? Did he show off before and after pictures of his most heinous cases to his undertaker friends? What must it be like to draw the blood out of a man when he's done using it in this life?

"Do you have a photograph?" asked Johnson.

"Yes," Ray's mother said, "Yes, I do." She unsnapped the latch on her shiny black purse and drew out a dog-eared black-and-white. It was an old photo. In the picture Ray's father was leaning up against the fender of a car. It was an old car, a classic, someone else's car. Ray's father was posing as if he owned the car, his hat tipped forward, his hands on his hips. "A fine-looking man," Johnson the undertaker said. "A large man."

"In his prime, yes," Ray's mother said.

"He has a fearless look about him," the undertaker said, holding the photo in the light cast by his desk lamp.

"Don't let it fool you," Ray's mother said. "It's just a picture."

The undertaker put the snapshot in a file folder. "Now," he said, "are there any other special details or arrangements you'd like me to prepare for?"

"Ray's going to read a poem," Ella said.

"I am?" Ray said.

"Yes you are," she said.

"All right then," said the undertaker. "Will that be at the wake or the funeral?"

"The funeral," said Ella. "Like a eulogy."

It was settled before Ray could protest. He would write a poem and read it at the funeral. He might write about eating rotten lettuce and waiting for his father in silence at the dinner table. Or he could write about how his father's face looked when he pressed a beer bottle to his lips and nursed. Or maybe Ray would try to describe the fearless look on his father's face in that photo the undertaker now had in his manila folder. All his life Ray's father wanted to be fearless, but something always got to him. That would make for a good poem maybe. Ray would call the poem

"Photograph of My Father in His Twenty-Second Year." It wouldn't be such a great eulogy perhaps, but who would fault Ray for it?

Johnson the undertaker did some final calculations and offered up a figure on a slip of paper. Ray's mother took the paper, read it, and nodded. This wasn't the sort of thing one haggled over, and anyway, Ella had never been much for haggling. She'd pay in cash up front before even a single vein was opened. From her purse she took out Ray's father's wallet. She held it in her hand like it was a museum piece.

The corners of the wallet were squashed like an accordion, the stitching frayed. The black leather had faded to gray in spots. The surface was scarred and the whole thing had retained the shape of Ray's father's ass—curved from being sat on day after day. Inside a wad of money bulged, waiting to be spent. Ray's mother slid the money out and handed it to Ray. His heart beat hard as he counted the bills and handed them over to Johnson.

Ray gave what was left back to his mother. She put the bills in the wallet, put the wallet back in her purse, and snapped the purse shut. Then she closed her eyes and sighed. Paid up. Paid in full. And the bastard would never walk through her door again.

According to Ray

The last time I saw Dick Nixon was in the hospital. He had had another phlebitis attack.

He looked like shit. Tubes coming out of him in every direction. Pat was feeding him ice cubes with her good hand when I walked in. "You look like shit," I said to Dick when Pat shuffled out of the room.

"You don't look so hot yourself," he said.

"I'm writing a poem right now in my head," I said, "and you're in it."

"It's about time," he said.

Then he wanted to know what the poem was about, so I told him. I said, "It has a morgue metaphor in it."

"Thanks a lot, asshole," he said.

"Don't mention it," I said. Then I told him some more about the poem. About how in the poem, he was quiet for once in his life. As quiet as the soft sizzle of snow.

"Lovely," Dick said.

"Silent and at peace," I said with a smirk.

Dick said, "Did you come here to cheer me up, you fucking idiot?"

"We get what we deserve, Dick."

We watched the television for a while then. Some documentary was on. Some public broadcasting show about archeology and architecture. When it was over, I could tell Dick was tired, so I said I'd be going.

That's when Dick reqested that I "stay the fuck away" from him. He said my face was gray. He said he'd seen it creep into people's faces before. He said I looked like Harold the summer before he kicked off. He said he just couldn't take it. "Too much sickness," he said. "I can't fight it anymore."

So that was it. I wasn't about to disobey the President's request. As I was leaving the room, he closed his eyes, but he wasn't asleep. He looked like a king lying there, waiting for somebody to come fan him with a palm branch. I never saw him again.

Condolences

Dear Beth,

Your husband was an asshole. Just like all the rest of us. No one knows that better than a wife. Now the bastard's up and died on us, leaving us to wonder what kind of hell this is that we're allowed to stay in it without him.

Of course you know, asshole or not, Ray Carver was the best damn fisherman I ever knew. Ain't a damn thing biting now that he's gone. So why am I telling you this? I don't know. I guess I want to say I could kill that son-of-a-bitch for leaving this earth without me. Can you imagine the salmon up in heaven? He's probably up there right now, hooking the biggest damn worm you ever saw onto the end of his line and casting it out into a crystal pond stocked full of God's finest. And here we are with nothing to do but wait.

I've been dead a few times already. My problem is I don't have the sense to stay dead. Some of these psycho-historian mother fuckers say the reason I screwed up my career is because of my fear of death. Maybe that's true. But now that Ray's gone, I'm starting to feel a little envious of the ones who know how to stay dead with dignity. Maybe I'm afraid to die because I know what the living will say about me when I'm gone, so I keep coming back to life to try and straighten the mess out.

You remember that damn poem of Ray's, the one called "In the Year 2020?" You remember that line about the famous dead? And that shit about how those we leave behind will talk about us like an old leaky faucet dripping away? Respectful and touched is what I think he said their talk would be when they found themselves haunted by our names, and the memories of what we did together. I'm paraphrasing because I don't have the damn thing in front of me. But I'm sure you remember it. Can you believe the gall of that asshole? Imagining himself beloved before he's even dead. That's a poet for you. No offense, but what a cock sucker.

And yet here I am stirred by the bastard's words anyway. For that matter, I'm stirred by just having known him. The mere mention of his name does make me smile. I was very lucky to have known him, Beth. Luckier than I deserved to be, as you very well know. Do me a favor, when you run into him on the shore of some heavenly lake, tell him I was grateful for his company.

I'm sorry for your loss. Sorry too that I couldn't make the funeral, but I think it was for the best that I not be there.

Dick

According to Himself

Look, you tell people RN grew up poor. You tell them he had
two brothers who died. You say, "RN played violin and piano,
football and soccer. RN was a champion debater and a religious
lad, a boy genius, an honest, hardworking, loyal, passionate, pa-
triotic youth." The people hear these things, and by and large,
they believe them because they want to believe in *something* for
God's sake. So they go to the polls and they register and they vote
for the man they believe in.

So you say, "RN listened to the train whistle at night and
dreamed of better places, greater frontiers, braver hopes." And the
crowd cheers and cheers and eventually when this happens, you
start to believe all of this stuff yourself until some smug bastard
says, "Hey, there weren't no Sante Fe line running through that
part of Whittier, California, in the 1930s—where do you get off
making up something like that, you lying sack of shit?!"

You're off guard, you can't remember how to slip the right
cross and parry with a jab. They can see the fluster in the whites
of your eyes. But you're RN, and this putz is nobody, so you blurt
out, "Fuck you, I oughta know what the hell I could hear outside
my own damn window, and I say it was the Sante Fe train
whistle!"

But the damage is done. RN's character is in question. And
the defensive outburst only made matters worse. And the next

thing you know, some evil son of a bitch with nothing better to do tells a wicked, heinous tale about how you once had perverse, unholy dreams in which the winking asshole of your poor, sweet mother gave birth to blue winged creatures. And some other sick cocksucker tells about how you allegedly fucked a large green piece of farm equipment once, or twice. Of course you deny these insane accusations, but by then it's too late. The damage is done.

Now everyone wants to believe *these* stories. Something to believe is something to believe. And hell, a Quaker momma's anus is a lot more interesting than soccer and the grocery business. You deny and deny, and deny some more, but they say, "Ah, the little boy who cried wolf," and now you're beginning to wonder if the train really did whistle in the distance or if maybe you read that in a biography about Teddy Roosevelt and you wanted it to be true so bad that you adopted it for your very own, and if that's possible, well, then maybe you did fuck a tractor when all that adolescent crap ran amok in your scrotum, and maybe you did even envision butterflies or bluebirds, or whatever, fluttering out of Hannah's asshole. Who knows? Maybe everyone envisions such things at one point or another. Who knows, indeed.

Of course, there will be those who will say, "Oh that's all just gobbledygook, flimflam, charades meant to confuse the already oppressed masses who deserve better. I mean, who would know RN better than RN himself, right?" Wrong. Let me just say this, and let me be perfectly clear on this, RN doesn't know RN any better than anybody else. Nobody knows. Not even me.

Go into a bar sometime. Or a grocery store anywhere in America. Or a classroom. Mention my name. See what happens. Everybody's got a Nixon story. Everybody has some little myth they've remembered all these years. They'll say, "Nixon's father ordered their house out of a Sears catalog," or "Nixon's family was in the grocery business," or "Nixon prayed to pictures of Abraham Lincoln," or "His mother was a Quaker," or "He called up NFL coaches and suggested plays." It's all a bunch of useless crap, but they remember it like it happened to them, like it's part of *their* biography.

And after they tell you whatever mythical facts they can recall about Dick Nixon, you can be sure they'll tell you what they think of him. Everybody's got an opinion. Most of them will say they hate the bastard. "He should have done time, they should have strapped him into the electric chair," they'll say. Some might say, "He got screwed, the poor son of a bitch." But I guarantee you every one of them will have an unalterable opinion. And the most important thing to remember is that whether they love me or hate me, almost all of the dumb slobs voted for me.

When RN leaves the earth, I'll leave it knowing that no matter what I did in my lifetime, no matter who I wronged, when the lights went out one last time, I was still the man who was once elected to the presidency by one of the largest landslides in the history of American politics. That's what I'll think of when I lie in my bed of ashes waiting for morning. That's what matters. And nothing can erase it.

It's a hell of a long way from Yorba Linda to the White House. But I made it. Imagine it. Millions of people standing in their voting booths at polling places all around the country. They're certain and confident as they reach up and push the button with the Nixon name on it. All over America, at the same time, voting machines click their approval. And at the end of the night, when the votes are tallied, Dick Nixon is the leader of the free world. He may be forever tarnished, but he's forever shining too. Dick Nixon *is* the fucking American Dream.

The last laugh is all mine. I stood on the edge of a swampy pond on Election Day and threw everybody in—my father, my brother, Vera Louise, Jack Kennedy, the whole damn country— and they squirmed and slithered in the muck, and I just laughed a big hearty Nixon cackle. If you listen, you can hear it echoing to this day.

According to Me

My mother cried the night President Nixon resigned. She didn't even like him. She had voted for McGovern—thought Nixon was an asshole actually. I remember asking her why she was crying and she said, "This is a sad day."

My father, on the other hand, sat in front of the TV going, "That SOB lied to our faces. That jag bag lied right through his goddamn teeth!"

I remember after the resignation speech, a reporter on the TV interviewed people at Disneyland to ask them what they thought should be done about Nixon. They were standing in line for some ride—Pirates of the Caribbean or It's a Small World I think. The reporter said something like, "Now that the truth is out, do you think Nixon should go to jail?" It was unanimous. "Fry the bastard," they all said.

I don't remember going to bed that night, but as I think about it now I suppose I probably lay awake for a while wondering about Nixon in the way I wondered about Santa Claus as a kid. I used to tell myself if I stayed awake long enough on Christmas Eve, I might hear Santa's reindeer on the roof, and then I'd know for sure that I could believe in him after all.

I suppose the truth of it is that I probably just lay there in my underwear sweating and listening to the sound of the highway howling off in the distance the same way Dick used to listen to that Sante Fe train.

I remember the first time I stumbled upon Ray Carver's last book of poems. It was on Dick's bookshelf. The copy was worn and tattered. There was a picture on the front of the book of two salmon swimming upstream into an oncoming wave. One of the fish seemed to be following the other. Something about the curve of the leader's tail made him look sure of where he was going but a little concerned about their destination, as if he knew there was a great white polar bear around the next bend, waiting for both of them. The follower looked wide-eyed, clueless, but trusting, and happy to follow.

I turned the book over in my hands, examining its broken spine, its dog-eared pages. Then before I even realized what I was doing, I had for some reason opened up the book to the very last page. I wanted to read the poem there, but I didn't dare. Instead, I held the book at arm's length and blurred my eyes in the direction of Carver's farewell to the world. There were answers on that page, in those blurry black ants marching across that white landscape, but I was still too afraid to find out what they were at that point, so I just closed the book and set it back on Nixon's shelf.

One night about a year after Ray died, Dick came over to listen to some music at my humble little midwestern bungalow. He brought his favorite Mahler record and told me to cue it up. Outside, determined summer cicadas droned on endlessly. Even the Mahler couldn't completely drown them out.

It was a particularly steamy August evening and the cicadas, having survived in great numbers due to a mild winter, were louder and more annoying than usual. I've been told cicadas never eat. They spend their short lives dodging hungry sparrows and buzzing their desperate mating calls late into the humid nights until they fuck their brains out, fall from the bark to which they cling, and then finally die in the mulch below—a hollow shell of their former selves. It's either fuck or be eaten. That's the life of a summertime cicada, cousin of the seventeen-year locust and brother to the June bugs that hurl themselves at your screen door long past June in the fading months that lead to the Midwest's inevitable, annual death.

That was the night Dick told me about how the girls in his school used to call him Gloomy Gus when he was a kid. He looked me right in the eye and said, "I deserved it, you know. I was a Gloomy Gus."

You could tell it was still eating him up, all these years later. But after he confessed his gloominess to me, he got this sneaky little grin on his face and he told me about how he once ate a handful of raw garlic cloves and then walked around his classroom breathing into the faces of all the girls who ever called him Gloomy Gus.

I forget who it was, but somebody once said, "Dick Nixon was the saddest man I ever knew." Sometimes I think that's the only true thing anybody's *ever* said about him. Sadness is the only thing left in the end.

After he told me the Gloomy Gus Eats Raw Garlic story, Dick asked me out of the blue, "What about you, kid? What's your story?" I have to admit, the question threw me. Asking questions wasn't the kind of thing Dick did very often. I was usually the one who asked the questions. Me or sometimes Ray. But now here was Dick asking me what my story was. As if all of a sudden now I could somehow manage to tell him *my* story.

I thought about telling him the story of my drunken father who punched holes in the walls of our house when I was a kid. Wall by wall, that house could tell a few stories of its own. I thought about telling Dick about the time my old man waved his .38 around, threatening to kill himself because my mother wouldn't give him the sex he required. I thought about telling him about the brother I never met—the one who died from some rare heart defect before I was born. If not for his death, I'd tell Dick, I might not have ever been born. Dick would like that angle. Or I could tell him about my mother's nervous breakdown and the insulin shock therapy she'd received in the hospital. Or my sister's meningitis and later her anorexia nervosa and general paranoia. I thought about telling him about the bubbleheaded bimbo I proposed to when I was eighteen, and how she slept with my British roommate when I went home for Thanksgiving. It would take a while, all these chapters in the saga of *my story*, but eventually I'd get to the part about how someday I was going to grow up to be a great writer or musician or archaeologist or comedian, somebody who people would remember.

But thinking about it all, one scene piled up on the others like that, made me wonder what the point would be of telling Dick all this. After all, it was a story he'd heard before. Same old, same old. So I just started to say, "Dick, you know, I don't have a story of my own," but just then the record ended and the needle got stuck. It was going around and around in the ungrooved center of the record, bouncing off the label, so I got up to change it manually, and when I turned around to ask Dick what he wanted to listen to next, he was gone. Just like that. Zap. Like *I Dream of Jeannie* or something. Gone. Maybe he slipped out the window. Who knows, maybe he just snapped his damn fingers, said "Shazam," and vanished. I guess it doesn't really matter where he went. The point is, that was the last I ever saw of him.

Outside, the cicadas droned to a standstill and finally stopped buzzing. Fucked out or eaten up, I don't know which, but for once, they were as silent as winter.

bibliography

Abrahamsen, David. *Nixon v. Nixon: An Emotional Tragedy*. New York: Farrar, Strauss and Giroux, 1977.

Adelman, Bob. *Carver Country: The World of Raymond Carver*. New York: Arcade Publishing, 1990.

Aitken, Jonathan. *Nixon, A Life*. Washington, D.C.: Regnery Publishing, Inc., 1993.

Ambrose, Stephen E. *Nixon*. New York: Simon and Schuster, 1987.

Carver, Raymond. *Fires*. New York: Vintage Books, 1984.

——————————. *A New Path to the Waterfall*. New York: The Atlantic Monthly Press, 1989.

——————————. *No Heroics Please*. New York: Vintage Books, 1991.

——————————. *Ultramarine*. New York: Vintage Books, 1986.

——————————. *Where Water Comes Together with Other Water*. New York: Random House, 1984.

David, Lester. *The Lonely Lady of San Clemente*. New York: Thomas Y. Crowell, Publishers, 1978.

Eisenhower, Julie. *Pat Nixon*. New York: Simon and Schuster, Inc., 1986.

Halpert, Sam. *. . . when we talk about Raymond Carver*. Layton, Utah: Gibbs Smith, 1991.

Henderson, Charles. *The Nixon Theology*. New York: Harper & Row, 1972.

Keogh, James. *This is Nixon*. New York: Putnam, 1956.

Kornitzer, Bela. *The Real Nixon*. New York: Rand McNally, 1960.

McGinnis, Joe. *The Selling of the President*. New York: Pocket Books, 1968.

Mazlish, Bruce. *In Search of Nixon*. New York: Basic Books, 1972.

Mazo, Earl and Stephen Hess. *Nixon: A Political Portrait*. New York: Harper & Row, 1968.

Nixon, Richard. *RN: The Memoirs of Richard Nixon*. New York: Simon and Schuster, 1990.

Osborne. *The Nixon Watch*. New York: Live Right, 1970.

Oudes, Bruce. *From: The President*. New York: Harper & Row, 1989.

Schulte, Renee. *The Young Nixon: An Oral Inquiry*. Fullerton: California State University Press, 1978.

Stull, William L. and Maureen P. Carroll. *Remembering Ray*. Santa Barbara: Capra Press, 1993.

Wills, Garry. *Nixon Agonistes*. Boston: Houghton Mifflin, 1970.

Witcover, Jules. *The Resurrection of Richard Nixon*. New York: Putnam, 1970.